ONLY THE BEGINNING

BY

MARIA ASHEN

THANK YOU IS A HUMBLE WORD

Justin Jay Gladstone.
This book and the coming series would not be possible if it weren't for him. He has been my biggest supporter, and he had faith in me and my work in the moments where I doubted myself the most. He is my writing coach, but most importantly, he is my friend – a friend who will always be there and have faith in me until the end. I am forever grateful for your cheering person, the countless hours you listened to me, and all the million hours we used on crafting this incredible story.

Our Writing Group.

Jay and I expanded our crazy team with two other incredible creators. They can write, draw, and create beautiful work. I love to have a pocket-sized team, and they are always only one message or call away to give their best and honest feedback. Thank you for your always-helping hands and extra eyes.

Danielle Novotny.

The Editor – Thank you so much for helping me with the typos and the grammatical aspects.

THE BETA READERS

Ime Atakpa.
You took the time to read through the story
and give me a lot of good notes that changed my
story into something that was much better than
before you laid your eyes on it.

Emily Quinn. Madelyn Grey. Lanie
Mores. Rebecca Amiss. Megan Harris.
Thank you for being the first ones who read
Only the Beginning, giving honest and
useful feedback which made the story way better
than it was.

FAMILY AND FRIENDS

Anne Mogensen. Ida, Nadia & Pia Hansen. Thank you for always supporting all my crazy ideas, no matter what you might think of this crazy career. You are always by my side.

THE ALPHA READERS

Isa & Taylor Eden.
Thank you for providing me with ideas of the finishing touches, which shaped the story into a completed piece.

CONTENT WARNING

This book contains content that might be
troubling to some readers: Visual description
of a violent nature.

A GUIDELINE

Throughout this book, you will find various
Spells spoken in the language of Kyra
and Raky. This symbol (») will provide
you with the instant translation.

A PRONUNCIATION GUIDE.

NAMES

HYPERION. –   HI-PE-RI-ON.

PERSEPHONE. –   PER-SEPHO-NE.

PEMPHREDO. –   PEM-FRE-DO.

ENYO. –   EN-YO.

DEINO. –   DE-I-NO.

THE GRAEAES. – THE-GRAY-ERS.

OLYSIA. –   O-LI-SIA.

SERENDIA. –   SE-REN-DIA.

HESTIA. –   HES-TI-A.

THE ALL-SEEING SIGHT INSTRUCTIONS:

DO NOT ALLOW THE SIGHT TO FOOL THE MIND.
EVERYTHING YOU SEE IS WHAT HAS HAPPENED, WHAT IS
HAPPENING AND WHAT WILL HAPPEN.

THE SIGHT RUNS ON THE BLOOD OF THE CREATOR.
NONE OTHER THAN THE BLOODLINE OF THEE, CAN
WHEEL THE POWER OF SIGHT.

IT SEES EVERYTHING WITHIN PAST, PRESENT AND FUTURE.
IT CANNOT AFFECT TIME.

THE SIGHT SPAN HAS NO LIMITATIONS WITH THE THREE
REALMS, GRANTING THE KEEPER THE GIFT TO LOOK
BEYOND TIME AND DISTANCE.

Table of Content

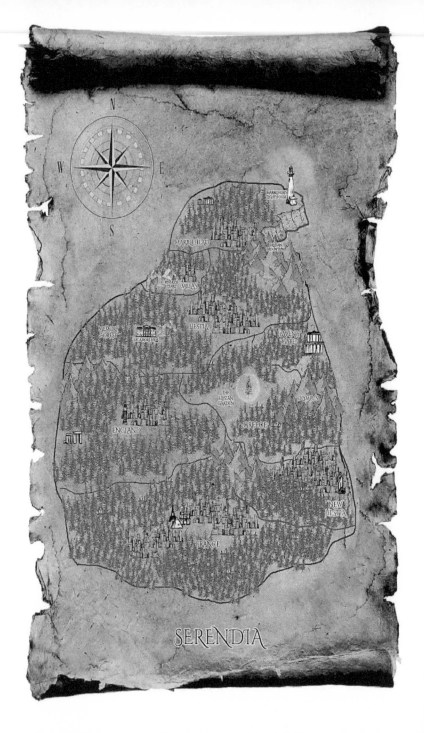

SERENDIA

*I*t began in 1690 with a *Pomegranate Flower.*
The wind danced playfully with the bottom of my long, green cloak. I strolled into my beloved gardens. The eternal spread of green bushes, the kaleidoscope of hydrangeas, trees that reached forth to the *Heavens*, and last but not least, the beaming life of the protected *Sacred Tree.* As the proud *Ruler of Earth*, I adored my wonders, which I had ruled for centuries.

I walked its many green valleys, bathed in its clear waters, stood at the top of the highest mountains, ventured into the depths of its numerous caves, and had seen every corner of the beauty that it held. But nothing could be compared to what I discovered in my gardens on that very day.

A hum, the choir of a million angels, was what first captured my attention. It was as though the wind carried it to my presence. And in the middle of my flowering surroundings, she stood.

Her auburn hair danced gracefully in the wind as a white gown wrapped around her fragile body and touched the ground. Her pale, beautiful face turned, and for the very first time I saw her honey-brown eyes, which shone like glittery sunlight.

She jumped back, frightened by my sudden approach. I placed a humble hand on my green-clothed chest, bowing my head. My long black hair framed my handsome face as my gleaming green eyes lifted to her.

"My lady, I did not mean to frighten you... I am Hyperion, The Ruler of the wonder that is this Earth." I slowly reached my hand toward her.

A smile sneaked onto her rosy red lips.

There at my feet sprouted the beautiful blossom of a pomegranate flower. Wide red, silky petals and a golden bud glimmered, just like her eyes in the sunlight. With careful movements, I bowed down, picked the flower gracefully, and extended it toward her. She accepted it, peeking over the red petals of the flower.

"Hello, mysterious Hyperion... My name is Persephone." She reached out her hand as my fingers wrapped around the silkiness of hers. My lips brushed the top of her hand in the gentlest of touches.

A flash of fleeting images sped across my mind. Beautiful Persephone in a white wedding gown granting me her every love. Walks in nature in a flood of happiness that I never experienced before. The perfect and innocent laughter of children, running around in my beloved gardens.

I lifted my eyes to her in awe. Her soft hand beamed with warmth in mine.

"Why have I never seen you in my beloved gardens?" Curiosity grew in my eyes; in a heartbeat our eyes met.

"Hmm, you see, I do not reside near here..." Persephone stated with a shy voice.

"Where do you reside?" Intrigue filled my throat, and I struggled to form a breath in pure excitement.

"Above." Her eyes lifted to the sky.

"Above...?" I repeated. "In Olympus?"

She nodded shyly. "My mother can be very... protective. I am only allowed to wander the grounds of

Earth in the *Spring* and *Summer*. Mother says I bring out the beauty of the world. I mustn't fall into the darkness of autumn or the cruelty of winter." Persephone had a look of longing in her eyes.

"Ah, I see... Well, that is certainly a shame. Those seasons hold just as much beauty as the others." My heart flickered like the beams of fireflies; never had I seen or encountered such a beautiful and warm soul.

"I am not sure my mother would agree." Persephone lifted her eyes to the sky as if she were being watched. Her eyes fell back to me with dread.

"Perhaps we should prove her wrong." I watched as an intriguing smile curved on Persephone's lips.

"And how do you suppose we would do such a thing?" Her voice rose with curiosity.

"The dusk of *Summer* is almost upon us... I could provide you with comfort and protection in my humble home. My temple reaches high above the nature of *Haven Gates*, and from there you could safely see the beauty of which I speak," I suggested with a glimmer of hope in my voice.

"I am not sure she would allow such abnormal behavior. The *Winter Solstice* is the last time I will step on this *Earth* before the darkness steals the light, and all life withers away," Persephone stated faintly.

"If I could only show you that it is the cycle of life. Life will wither for new life to be born..." I held her hand a bit too tight in excitement. "Let me speak to your mother, and I shall convince her of your safety in my temple. I will personally see to your return... Call upon her, my sweet Persephone... I will convince her of the adventures that could lie ahead of you."

Persephone's eyes glimmered with excitement as she smelled the flower. The wind danced playfully with her auburn hair, and the suns in her eyes intensified.

"A world beyond my own would be a wonderful sight, I am certain..." She nodded looking to the sky. "I will summon her."

Persephone smiled, turned around, and stepped into the openness of the garden. She sat down and laid the flower with a lifted head. Her eyes closed; taking a deep breath, a breeze blew across her pale face. Her fiery hair danced gracefully around her.

"Mitéra, akoúo mea klísi. Veni pros to mea." »

(Mother, I call upon thee. Come to me).

The wind blew harder, and a shiny light crossed the sky, beaming gracefully down in front of her. The light faded, and a tall, pale goddess stood before her wearing a silver gown and a golden crown of leaves and flowers. Her ocean-blue eyes fell on Persephone, and a smile spread on her almost white lips. Grace shone from her as she looked upon her daughter.

"Mea filia... You called upon me." Her mother's smile faded as her narrowed eyes lifted to me. "Hyperion." She carried a confidence that caused a shake to unwillingly begin in my hands. She towered frighteningly before me.

I cleared my throat, sensing how I was stepping onto a battlefield of a million soldiers, waiting to slay me. "Demeter, Goddess of Harvest and Fertility, once again we stand before each other," I offered respectfully.

"Unwillingly... We do not speak of you at *Olympus*... Well, that is not entirely true. You are known as the free spirit who felt too mighty to rule amongst his *own* kind," Demeter said with spite.

"The *Earth* called to me. Here I can have it all, instead of living in the shadows of my brother, Zeus."

Demeter ignored my remark and glanced at her daughter. "What are you doing in the presence of *my* Persephone?" Demeter wondered as Persephone rose to her feet.

"I have a request, glorious Demeter. A beauty such as your daughter deserves to see the world in all its glory, and since she has only seen the wonders of *Spring* and *Summer*, I offered her a protected spot in my temple, where she can look upon the palette of colors that *Autumn* and *Winter* will bring. She will be within the protection of my *Graeaes*."

"Absolutely not!" Demeter roared.

"But mother—"

Demeter held up her hand, stopping Persephone before she could continue. Tears pooled in her glittery honey eyes.

"I assure you, Demeter, she will be perfectly safe. I will make sure of it," I insisted with all the control and respect I could muster.

"A simple *Shadow God* like you cannot protect her from the death and darkness that *Winter* holds. She is far too fragile and beautiful to be exposed to such profanities... Persephone, your glory days are over for this year. Return at once to *Olympus*," Demeter demanded.

"I will see you again, I am certain of this!" I caught Persephone's eyes before she beamed away in a white light, and just like that, she vanished from my presence.

Demeter pierced me with her eyes. "You are never to go near or even speak to my daughter! If you do, I will make the wrath of your brother come crashing down upon you." In the same shiny beam, Demeter returned to *Olympus*.

With my powers a green cloud formed around me, and in a rush, I appeared within the high, marble walls of my mighty Temple. I dragged myself over the shiny, sandy marble floors and crumpled down in my high-backed throne of gold.

The view of white columns and sun-catching chandeliers seemed to fade compared to what I had seen in my gardens. I sighed deeply. Clear of mind, and empty at heart.

"Hypi, are you alright?" Soft voices like the choir of angels approached me.

"I am in despair, ladies." I looked upon the three *Graeaes* in front of me, each more glorious than the next.

"What has happened?" Pemphredo wondered with a broken voice and purple eyes of wonder, which mirrored her long purple gown. She bowed her head, and curly rose-red hair fell in front of her pale face.

"I saw the most beautiful girl... No offence to you, of course. I offered her the chance to spend the winter days in my company..." I hoarsely sighed, taking Pemphredo's soft, peachy hand.

"And she refused?" Enyo wondered as tears pressed in her jade-green eyes, and she gripped tightly at the fall of her flowering pear-green dress.

I stroked her pale cheek, brushing her caramel brown hair behind her ear. "No, she wanted to join me... But her mother, Goddess Demeter, refused to let her spend another second on my *Earth*... I had just hoped to show her some of the beauty I brought you into as well."

Pemphredo placed a caring hand on my arm.

"Hypi, when you rescued us from a destiny worse than death, we promised to do anything we could to make you happy... But here we feel powerless." Deino fell into the arms of Enyo, who stroked Deino's curly blonde hair. Deino's magnetic-blue eyes fell on me with despair. She grabbed the corner of her light blue gown and pulled wildly at its length to dry her eyes.

"I am afraid you are... No one would be wise enough to stand up against a Goddess. I am not looking for trouble, ladies. Only someone who could make my heart flow with joy," I stated.

"And did she?" Deino wondered with a smile which appeared behind the blue shield of her dress.

I nodded and bowed my head. "Yes, she did..." A smile forced its way through. "I got this fleeting glimpse of the future we will have..."

"Well, perhaps there is a way we can make her return," Enyo offered, which caught Pemphredo's attention.

"Yes, you spoke of your visions... There must be a way to bring her here," Pemphredo suggested.

"Some spell perhaps?" Deino suggested with the hint of a smile, nodding.

"Oh no, my ladies... I will not turn to such ways." I insisted strongly.

"Oh, I see... Well, perhaps, we can find something to ease your mind?" Enyo wondered. My attention turned to her, nodding.

"Perhaps one of the divine herbal teas, my sweet?" I suggested, smiling at Enyo.

A loud banging sounded on the tall wooden doors of the Temple which caught my attention. I lifted my head in surprise as I heard the doors creak open.

"Hyperion, someone is at the door for you." Charon requested my presence. He stood straight in his green tuxedo and held the door.

I walked to him, placing a hand on his shoulder and nodding respectfully. "Thank you, old friend." I stepped to the door and gauged my hallway.

And there, in the frames of stone columns and wooden carvings, she stood. As beautiful as I remembered her from the moments in the garden.

"Persephone... You are here." The air left my mouth, and for a moment I could not believe it.

"Nothing can stop me from seeing new adventures, not even the wrath of Zeus. I wish to spend the *Winter* days in your arms and see everything your *Earth* has to offer." Persephone reached her arm toward me.

My eyes were glued to hers with a smile. A chill of shock replaced my happiness as my eyes fell on her hand. Red and violet bruises wrapped around her wrist, like a bracelet of pain.

"Did she hurt you?" Persephone's eyes escaped to the floor. "Why have your wounds not healed?"

"Mother wanted to make sure she would be the only one to help me in life... She placed a *Healing Blockage* on me. I am not to be healed by any account but hers." Persephone's voice grew shy as tears gleamed in her eyes.

"Enyo, be a dear and collect one of your cooling herbs, would you, my sweetness?"

"Certainly." My eyes spotted Enyo retrieve the herbs from the room before I gazed back.

"Do not worry, my dear Persephone. You will be in good hands with my *Graeaes*." I winked and a flood of warmth pulsated through my body. My eyes fell to her rosy lips, and my heart pounded.

"Here you go, miss Persephone." Enyo reached out, carefully taking Persephone's wounded hand, and with the other she made a green wrap around the bruises with a mix of *Sage Leaves* and *Thyme Ribbons*.

"Thank you, you are too kind." Persephone searched me momentarily with her eyes.

"No trouble at all, miss." The ladies shared a smile.

I held my arm toward Persephone, and she accepted.

"PERSEPHONE, COME FORTH!" A roar bellowed outside the door so loud it shook the walls. Despair formed in Persephone's frightened eyes.

I gazed into her eyes and placed my hands on her cheeks. "Do not worry, I will talk to her." She mirrored my nod. We stepped to the door, and Charon pulled it open.

Demeter stood on the landing of the stairs and seemed to tower higher than before. Anger had replaced her ocean eyes with crimson pearls of hate. Persephone released my arm and swooped behind me. I approached the first step.

"Persephone, do not hide behind that traitor. Release her now, *Shadow God*!" Demeter raged.

"No one is keeping her here against her will, and neither should you!" Demeter's eyes shot wider and her pale features flared pink with rage.

"Mind your tongue, Hyperion!" In an instant her demeanor changed, and she raised her chin high in a headshake. Then her downturned mouth formed a vicious smile. "Very well... You chose not to obey me... Persepy, you disappoint your mother."

Persephone stepped a bit closer and held her wounded hand with care.

Laughter spread from Demeter as she observed the herb wrap. "Puny tricks, I see. No one shall heal you like me. No one shall house you like me. And no one should dare stand against me." Demeter shook her head back and forth, almost in slow motion. She bit her bottom lip with narrowed eyes. "Are the filthy *Graeae* not enough to satisfy your disgusting needs?" Demeter crooned.

A chill of shock rippled through me, and nausea watered my mouth as I took another step down. "Oh my... No, no... I would never... The *Graeae* are like my children. I would never lay with them! You are standing at my door, offending me and my ladies. How dare you?" My heart raged like wild horses.

"Oh, one can never be too sure of your ways. You are a traitor to your own kind, after all." She tilted her head with lifted eyebrows. Her flowery crown glistened in the sun – a beauty with such a cruel heart.

For a moment, I could do nothing but feel sorry for her. Taking a deep breath, I took another step down. "I am fairly sure the other Gods do not see me in such a way," I insisted strongly and looked upon her towering figure.

One of her brows lifted this time. "Well, you could go ask them yourself... Oh, but no... You value yourself too highly to travel to such divine places, I presume." She placed her hands on her back and turned her side to me as she gazed upon Persephone with a malevolent stare. Her eyes had turned back to the ocean blue, and it was then I realized that a much more sinister and cunning look hid beneath the beauty.

"Very well..." She nodded and stepped all the way in front of me. Her hand grabbed tightly around my muscular arm as her red nails drilled into my skin. "You can have her for now!" she declared, moving her cheek next to mine. "But mark my words, *Shadow*..."

I sensed her warm breath on my cheek, which prickled uncomfortably.

"Giving in so easily?" I spat back in spite with narrowed eyes to no amusement but my own.

"Enjoy your time with her. She will tire of the simplicity of your ways, and you cannot provide her with the company of like-minded and equally powered beings like *Olympus* holds. You have chosen your simple destiny; why lure her down with you? You are a pitiful God. Only the shadows are worthy of your tiresome company." Her grip faded from my arm, and she stepped back. Her eyes locked on Persephone.

"I will see you again shortly, my darling... Enjoy the simplicity of his world!" Demeter was engulfed in a bright light which beamed forth to the heavens.

In haste I ran to Persephone's side, wrapping my arms around her. As I held her closely, my heart pounded wildly, and my eyes searched the white clouded sky. A paranoia was created in me: *Would she return in the shadows of the night to steal Persephone?*

"You are safe now." I heard my own voice break into uncertainty. "Demeter will never be in our way; she will never stop us. The future is set in stone, so we are safe," I assured her.

My grip loosened, but she remained in my embrace. I placed a hand on her cheek, and my thumb stopped the fall of a tear. I sunk into the suns of her honey-brown eyes. My heart throbbed with excitement as my eyes fell on her lips.

"My Temple will be your home for however long you please." A smile made her watery eyes curve with joy.

I placed my hand on her back with care as I pulled her closer.

Pemphredo, Enyo and Deino gathered around us, all of them adoring her with a smile in their eyes.

"Welcome to your new home, miss," Pemphredo stated with a warm smile on her pale face.

Enyo reached out, softly touching Persephone's arm. "Another sister has joined our family."

Persephone's eyes shone with a light I had rarely seen.

Enyo moved gracefully to the piano playing angelic tunes as Deino stood by singing like a choir of angels. Pemphredo watched us all from her favorite seat in the wide window bay, and every now and then a smile spread on her pink lips. Like had she forgotten to shelter her emotions, only for a tiny moment, and the whole universe shone from her eyes.

It was then my eyes glided down to Persephone in my embrace. My head bowed down to hers, and for the first time my lips met with the softness of hers. An electric boost of energy flooded me. I would never want her to leave.

This kiss was the first of many, and it was a kiss that sealed our lives under the *Harvest Full Moon*, and she was crowned *My Queen of Earth.*

Finally, throughout all my centuries of ruling this *Earth*, I had found my heart's desire. My beautiful Persephone, to whom I would give my world. My temple was completed with yet another beauty.

My beautiful queen was adored just as much by my beloved *Graeaes.* Deino and Enyo sat by the beautiful grand piano, filling the room with wonderful tunes. Pemphredo's reflection was mirrored on the surface of the black piano as she sung the vocals of angels. Persephone adored my ladies with a wide smile on her face, and I could not take my eyes away from her.

She spread a sense of joy and family, of which I had never felt before. My eyes shortly fell on her wounds which had healed by the *Graeaes'* kindness and herbs, and she was welcomed into their lives as one of their own.

*D*emeter watched in dismay how her
daughter sunk into a world from which she would not
be able to pull her out. Every day she stood at the edge of
Olympus and gazed over the land she dreaded oh so
eternally, hoping that one day her daughter would return.

Persephone and I waltzed through a palette of
orange, brown, green, and red forests. A spread of colors
wrapped around us. The forest floors were covered with a
carpet of multicolored autumn leaves. Her fragile, pale
features stood out stunningly, and her auburn hair flamed
with a shine that took my breath away.

"If this is what the death of autumn looks like, then
it is a beautiful way to perish!" Her statement made me
chuckle, and she smiled widely.

I adored her in the spread of colors: she was dressed in a gown that brushed the forest floor, and a white fur coat which dragged behind her. She had the innocence of a child, and a curiosity for *our Earth*.

"I am happy you like all of it, my darling." I placed a soft hand on her cheek, meeting her silky lips with my own. We chuckled in a kiss, and warmth spread deep within me. A ripple infected me with positivity, and for the first time in my life, my heart pounded with the rhythm of nature.

"Thank you for opening my eyes to all beauties of the seasons, my dearest Hyperion..." Her clear honey-brown eyes shone as her red lips curved into a smile.

The *Autumn* days turned into glittery snow and crystal-ice as Persephone saw the beauty of which I had spoken.

Snow covered the beauty of my beloved gardens, and I saw in Persephone's eyes how surprised she was. Her thin, glove-covered fingers caressed the frozen red roses which glittered in the sunlight, like perfect snowflakes.

"Mother was mistaken. This is... so... beautiful..." Persephone was out of breath, wrapping her warm fur coat around herself as a mist cloud revealed her warm breath in the cold. "And cold." She giggled as I wrapped my arm around her to try to keep her warm. Her cheeks were rosy, and her small nose was red.

A crunch in the snow revealed a presence, and we both turned as Pemphredo strolled by us. Persephone was surprised to see Pemphredo's bare feet stepping on the snow-covered ground. Her arms were bare, and her cheeks rosy.

"Are you not cold?" Persephone wondered.

"No, I feel no physical pain, miss," Pemphredo stated with the hint of a smile. Her purple eyes shone.

"Why...?" Persephone asked out of breath.

"That is an awfully long and dull story, miss... Maybe for another time? One when the cold wind does not bite at your beautiful face." The two ladies nodded, and Persephone's eyes turned to mine.

"Let us return to our beloved home, My King."

I guided her into the temple. The heat inside prickled on my cheeks, and I observed as Persephone shed her coat, and her long red hair swung in the air around her.

As she saw me, her eyes gleamed with joy, and the smile on her face sprouted with happiness. The kindness of Persephone melted my heart in those cold winter days.

Because the cold was too much for Persephone's fragile and beautiful face, I placed us in front of the fire, where we spoke of our future. My rough fingers wrapped around hers as the crackle of the fire played our lovely melody.

I placed a kiss on her rosy lips and my cheek by hers, whispering softly, "A beauty such as yours should be shared and spread. I want you to carry my child, my dear Persephone."

A smile of pure love formed on her face. A spread of glittering butterflies danced around her in a colorful mist that only I could see. It mimicked her beauty, and in that moment, I knew she wanted just the same.

"You and I, and a little one can grow my empire and create a successor for my legacy. For my *Earth* and for my *Graeaes*."

This was no ordinary tale of love and happiness.

Winter turned to *Spring*, the time of new life and new beginnings, and with that our want for a child grew stronger by the day.

When the sun rose on the first *Summer Day*, Persephone sunk into a state of despair and sadness. Although Persephone was the Goddess of Fertility and Vegetation, she could not conceive. Her fertility went to the *Earth*.

Still, the vision I had seen on the day that we met kept repeating in my mind, and I was certain of the future I had seen, because everything in the future was set in stone. The only question was, how would this unfold?

In the third month of her barrenness and despair, I encountered an idea I never thought I would have.

"Your mother has such great powers... Perhaps she can help us with our troubles," I carefully suggested.

"Mother does not approve of my choices, so I doubt she will ever lend us her help." Persephone sighed deeply as her eyes fell to the floor.

"My Queen, if only you would try, our sorrow would die, and our happiness could live on... What other choice do we have?" I persisted with a pleading voice.

"Very well, My King... I will do what you ask of me. However, only to ease this pain." Persephone's voice broke.

Sometime that following morning, Persephone ventured toward *The Elysian Gardens*. From a distance, I crept closer and watched as she sat in the natural elements of the garden and silently prayed for the appearance of her mother.

"Mitéra, akoúo mea klísi. Veni pros to mea." »
(Mother, I call upon thee. Come to me.)

The wind blew across her face, and her flaming hair danced around her. Her honey-brown eyes were lifted to the sky. A fleeting beam of light flashed to the ground, and Demeter appeared in front of her daughter.

"My daughter... Have you tired of his ways yet? Are you here to come home?" Hope built in Demeter's voice, but it vanished from her eyes as Persephone shook her head.

"Mother, I come to you begging for my heart's desire. We long for a child of love, beauty, and grace, but I cannot provide. I plead for your wisdom and help..."

Disapproval shone from Demeter's eyes as she shook her head with pouted lips. "I am ashamed of how low he has caused you to sink. No child should be bred by him. No more of him should walk this *Earth* or breathe the same air as I. You have chosen your own fate, my dear child. A life with him brings nothing but loneliness and heartache. Despite this being a power of mine, I shall not provide. My shame is boundless when I look at you by his side."

Demeter's cruel remarks shocked Persephone.

Anger ripped the air from my lungs as I clung to a tree branch by my side. I could not take the cruelty any longer, so I retreated to my Temple.

I sat in my throne and waited for hours on end for Persephone to return with the bad news I knew she carried. Finally, the door creaked open, and she entered.

Puffy red eyes were the first thing I saw on her swollen face. Our eyes met. She shook her head as tears trickled down her cheek, and she ran off to the chamber.

That starry summer night, I held her in my arms as she wept. Sadness such as this I had never encountered.

My heart broke from the helplessness I felt toward my grieving wife. *How would these visions come true? I would do anything in my power to make it so.*

"Oh, my beloved Hyperion, she refused to help us." Persephone's voice broke, and a knife pierced my heart from the sound of her pain-filled voice.

"We will find a way, I promise you, my sweet Queen. I will do whatever it takes." I squeezed her closer to me and held her with all the love I could muster.

Abruptly she turned away from me, and her breathing went heavy.

"This is all your fault!" she fired, turning. Her eyes were the same crimson pearls I had seen in her mother.

"My fault? How am I to blame for this?"

"You never should have stood against her. You doomed me to a life here, childless and barren," Persephone accused with a teary voice.

"These are the words of your mother," I insisted.

"Maybe she was right, after all. You did lure me down here!" A knife twisted in my heart.

"I did nothing of the sort!" My voice rose unwillingly.

"I wanted nothing but..." Her voice broke, and so did my heart. Tears burst through her eyes.

She lurched at me, pounding at my chest. I grabbed her cheeks in her hysteria.

"Mitescere, amina mea!" » *(Calm down, my love! – Ancient Calming Spell).*

In an instant, she went limp in my arms. The ancient spell had worked its magic.

I lifted her into my arms and carried her to bed. I watched my beloved fall into a deep sleep of devastation and despair. I stepped by her side, stroking her raspberry cheek, and bowed down to kiss her.

A glance over my shoulder made my eyes venture beyond the halls and land on the wooden door of my studies. With determined, heavy steps, I approached the door and grabbed the handle.

"Hypi?" I glanced once again over my shoulder, and to my surprise, my trustworthy *Graeaes* stood before me.

"Ladies?" My voice failed to hold the authority I tried to maintain.

"We implore you not to do what you think to do." Pemphredo stepped ahead of them and met her purple gleaming eyes with mine.

"I made her a promise!" I insisted, knowing in my heart it could lead to defeat.

"Nothing good will come of this!" Enyo insisted with her hypnotic green eyes. It was like all the power of nature gathered in her presence to stop me.

But my will was too strong. I ripped my gaze from hers and opened the door.

"There's nothing else left to do. I have seen the future. I will do everything to make it so!" I swooped inside the darkened room and left my beautiful oracles to their desperate thoughts.

The frame of my study was barely visible in the darkness. I lifted my arm in the direction of the misused fireplace and closed my eyes.

"Lux, mea via!" » *(Light, my way.)*

I sensed the flicker of light behind my eyelids. As I opened my eyes, my square room filled with dusty wooden shelves and ancient books seemed to close in on me. I stepped forward, breathed deeply, and reached for one particular book.

I grabbed it by the spine, prying it out. The surface shone upon me with a mocking light. Golden letters stood out to me, spelling out the word of light magic: *KYRA*. I sighed deeply, lifting my eyes to the ceiling.

"I am sorry, Hermil... But the light magic we crafted will not provide me with what I need." I placed the book back on the shelf as my hand moved to the book beside it. My hand slid across the surface, creating a finger trail in the dust over the title, *Ancient Blood Magic*.

The wooden chair creaked as I took a seat at the desk. I placed the book in front of me and carefully turned the delicate, slightly torn pages. Symbols of horror and death spread before me. It haunted my mind with a darkness I never thought I would see. I squeezed my eyes tightly with a deep sigh.

"Restrain yourself, your *Queen* desires this!" I slammed my fist into the table and reopened my eyes.

I turned a few more pages, and there it was. An image of a curled up, bloody fetus filled me with nausea. Above the image was a list of ingredients, along with a spell of approach.

The chair scraped on the floor as I pushed it back. Glass jars clinked against each other as I searched for the ingredients on one of the shelves. One by one they were placed on the table: *Belladonna Flower Seeds, Dried Bloodroot* and *Ashes...* I moved my finger over the list and stopped abruptly.

"In all holiness, this cannot be... *A Sacrifice of Life*."

Desperately I looked around the room for the smallest animal. Moonlight flooded through the window. In the corner of the window frame, a moth was desperately trying to escape, like it knew what its fate held in store.

I reached out, grabbed it, and crushed it quickly. A sense of sadness rushed over me as I placed the corpse of the moth in a wooden bowl with the rest of the ingredients.

The remaining element was blood of the person in question. The blade of my knife glistened in the moonlight as I held it to my palm. A sting followed the cut, and blood trickled into the bowl. The wound instantly healed.

I held a hand over the mixture, clearing my throat. "Ignis!" » *(Light a fire).*

A flame rose from the bowl, and the light glistened in my green eyes. I slid my finger across the written spell and took a deep breath, saying, "Ego exolvo mea dusé pro reditus autem nový vita. Solvo mea dusé tobé." » *(I give my soul for the return of new life. I release my soul to thee.)*

The flames burned out in an instant, and a sense of vertigo almost knocked me off my feet. I grabbed the bowl and drank the thick, sticky substance. The ashes were dry on my tongue, and everything tasted like metal and death.

I dried my mouth and threw the bowl into the fire. I reached for the book but was stopped by an excruciating burn in my arm, and with a heavy crack, the bone in my arm twisted and broke. A roar of pain escaped me as I fell to my knees and twisted in pain. The fire spread in my body; one by one the entirety of my bones broke, faster than I could heal. The crunches and cracks echoed in the room that swayed around me. My vision blurred, and the metallic taste of blood filled my mouth.

Bangs knocked on the door as the cries of my concerned *Graeaes* mixed with the cracks of bones. The pain paralyzed me with no chance of moving; I was nailed to the floor.

In my haze of dizziness and nausea, a ball of green light flooded out through my mouth, and I sensed how all warmth left my body.

The moonlight from the window shone brighter with a luring light, and I sensed how angels were calling out to me. The green beam of light danced around in the room like a firefly, until it finally vanished in the flames of the fireplace.

The moonlight faded, and the calls abruptly stopped. The flames flickered as a mass of blackness shaped like a skull rose within the fire. Chills infected my body, and a numbness possessed me. The blackness approached me, and with every breath I took, I was pierced with the splinters of my own bones. The mass entered my mouth as a tear ran down my face.

In a gasp, I was empowered with a strength I had never sensed before. My body was restored, and every bone healed instantly. I turned on my stomach, coughing violently. A pool of blood and black smudge was emptied from me. I dried my mouth, and I gently pushed myself up. The ground still swayed, so I grabbed the back of the chair and gained my balance.

The cries of my ladies sounded from the door. I threw a look of disgust at the book and closed it in a dust cloud, placing it back on the shelf.

As I pushed the door open, I found my three *Graeaes* on their knees, crying. They raised synchronically with fear painted on their perfect faces. The shine of purple, green, and blue eyes pierced me. With a sigh I stepped pass them.

"Hypi, do not do this," Enyo pleaded on her knees.

"No one shall keep me from laying with my wife, not even you!" I grunted more violently than intended. I stopped in my pursuit of the upstairs and bowed my head in shame. "I am sorry, my beauties, but this has to be done. The dark powers will help me reach my desires."

Even saying that sentence out loud, I knew exactly what kind of wrongs I had just committed. And what horrors I was further willing to commit.

Three

DOOMING DARKNESS

I That night I laid with my wife and silently prayed for my sacrifice to bear fruit. But it was not only the life of a moth I had sacrificed that night. Something stayed with me, something that gave me chills to the core of my now-darkened soul. I had turned myself over to a darker fate, and months passed without any fertility.

I stood at the balcony of our bed chambers and gazed upon the mighty mountains to my right where black majestic points of stone reached towards the sky. I bowed my head down as I gripped the stone rail before me. I squeezed tightly, and the stone gave way under my enormous strength.

"It should have worked!" I raged, grabbed a vase, and crashed it into the floor. It shattered into a million pieces. To my horror, Persephone stood before the spread of glass.

"Pardon me, my dearest... I did not mean to bre—"

"—What should have worked?" she wondered with worry painted all over her face.

"Nothing, my love..."

She directed her way carefully around the glass and grabbed my arms as she reached me. "Speak to me, Hyperion... What should have worked?"

In shame, my eyes fled hers. "I did something.... horrifying," I sighed as my head bowed down.

"What? What... did you do?" Her voice shook with fear, and her eyes watered.

"I did what I thought would bring a child to our home... But I failed," I sighed.

"Tell me what you did!" she insisted even stronger.

"I traded my soul for a child." I spoke words that weighed like stones.

Her hands covered her mouth as tears rolled from her gleaming eyes. "What have you done?" She backed away from me in horror. The glass crunched under her feet as it penetrated her fragile skin.

"Persephone, watch your step." I grabbed her, lifting her into my embrace. The glass crunched under my bare feet as well, but no pain followed, only a tiny prickle as I left a trail of bloody footprints.

She wouldn't even look at me as her face cringed from the pull of glass from her foot. I carefully wrapped her foot and searched her eyes.

"Pers, it is still me... I am still the same Hyperion. I beg of you... look at me."

Her face turned, and her eyes looked at me. But her look hurt more than the shards of glass in my feet. The suns in her eyes had burned out, and all that was left was a faded glow of honey.

After that day, Persephone drew deeper into herself, and spent her nights staring at the moon. I tried everything a loving husband would to make his wife uplifted again. But our childlessness drove a wedge between us.

Eventually love withered and faded, like a dying flower that no power on *Earth* could restore. Sadness stole the beautiful spirit Persephone once had, and I dreadfully watched how despair drew the life from her. Persephone would sit in Pemphredo's spot in the window bay staring aimlessly at the falling rain.

A warm hand touched my shoulder, which caused me to turn my eyes away from Persephone.

"Sire, neither of you seem happy anymore... What you did—"

"—Stop it, Pem!"

"Let me speak to her." Pemphredo strolled gracefully toward the bay, her purple gown flowered behind her. I watched her sit next to Persephone, and I turned my head, pretending not to listen to them.

Pemphredo reached out her hand, softly touching Persephone's, which made her eyes turn away from the rain. "My Queen..." Pemphredo's voice was distant from my view in the kitchen.

"Call me Persepy."

Pemphredo faked a smile, nodding. "I know what troubles you, however, do not let your love die. Hyperion loves you deeply... I am aware that he has been changing, but all he does and all that he has ever done is for you..." Pemphredo assured.

"It is too late, Pemphredo... My life does not make sense... I am the *Goddess of Fertility*, yet I will never carry a child." Persephone's voice broke, and she fell into Pemphredo's arms crying.

The sight of her devastation torched my soul like a burning fire poker, which vaguely affected me with any pain. Ultimately Persephone returned to *Olympus*, much to her mother's delight.

A sorrow stronger than time itself formed around my broken and torn-up heart. Left alone in the shadows of my former life with the *Graeaes* as my only company, the darkness stole the sense of the life I once knew. Yet I swore never to give up my dream of a family.

"This cannot be! My future was set in stone!" I hammered my hand into the table which created cracks. I had seen it all, and the future lay securely before me, just within reach and then... It was taken away.

My hand tightened into a fist, and my heartbeat raged like the flames of hell. And in that moment, it became painfully clear to me that I had traded my soul for nothing.

"Hyperion... There must be another way to achieve your heart's desire," Pemphredo proclaimed as she watched Enyo and Deino standing around our long dining-table.

"What about your study? Many of those ancient, dusty books must hold some answers," Enyo suggested.

"Perhaps Charon could retrieve some of them, and we could search them?" Deino wondered.

"Absolutely not... No one goes into my study but me!" I assured venturing to my study and grabbing the *Ancient Blood Magic* grimoire before returning to the dining-room. The book thumped onto the table, and I swung my green cloak to the side and took a seat. The *Graeaes* watched me flip open the dusty and powerful book.

"I sense darkness around this book..." Enyo stated, "How did you encounter it?"

I lifted my eyes from the pages. "Hermil Blake and I used to study magic together. We crafted the Spells of *Kyra* as well as the power of *Raky* within this one," I explained, which did not seem to quell any concern they might hold.

"Hypi... Are you certain of this? Look at what has already happened to you all because of that book!" Pemphredo insisted as the other ladies chimed in with agreement.

"Hypi... That name makes me sick. For this moment forward, you will only refer to me as Sire." Their eyes shone with sadness, but in that moment, I felt no sympathy towards them. "This may be my only solution..." I insisted. "Will you be my help or not?!" I hissed.

Their silence made me doubt all sense of helpfulness.

"Need I remind you, who helped and saved all of you? Gave you a chance when you needed it the most?!" My questions left them quieter. "Nothing?" I hissed.

"Certainly..." Deino said before Enyo had any chance to.

"Ladies, perhaps you will prepare a cup of tea for Hyperion, and I will help him search," Pemphredo demanded, and the other two ladies ventured to the kitchen. Pemphredo moved to my side, placing a hand on my shoulder. "Whatever you did in that study has changed you, Hyperion... You speak to those ladies with a tone that touches their soul..." Pemphredo's grip on my shoulder tightened. "What has happened to you?"

"I gave everything up to provide my queen with a child... And look what my soul sacrifice has done for me... I am left with you!" I mocked.

Her eyes narrowed. "You are not the man who saved us... Our Hyperion is fading by the day... Seeing where you are standing now, was it worth it?" Pemphredo questioned, but an answer was never provided because Enyo and Deino entered the room.

My eyes pierced through Pemphredo, and my blood boiled as an anger possessed me stronger than I had ever felt before.

A hand on my shoulder made my arm swing. It hit Deino's hand, knocking the cup from her hand, and the boiling tea burned into her arm. Pemphredo ran to her aid. A sinking feeling gripped hold of me as I heard the blood-curling scream from my beloved.

"Deino, I..." I stepped toward her.

She was sitting on a chair, and Pemphredo kneeled before her. I moved closer, but Pemphredo held up her hand.

"Do not come any closer!" Pemphredo commanded, and something in me froze. If it was her will or my despair, I was not sure.

Enyo placed a comforting hand on Deino's shoulder as Pemphredo carefully held her wounded arm, holding her soft right hand over the wound. "*Percuro!*" A purple light shed from her hand, and the wound began to heal.

Deino looked upon me with tear-filled eyes.

I fled to my chambers, watching the darkened sky and wondering what had become of me. Pemphredo was right; I was slipping from my prior self.

I wished for the day of Persephone's return, but later I would encounter that such a day would never come. Still, I clung to the hope of the visions I had seen, that somehow all of this would turn around, and my beloved Persephone would return to me and our childless days would be far behind us.

Day after day and century after century, I wandered into my beloved garden in hope that one day my beloved would return, so my visions would play out as I had seen them. But every day I would return to my Temple empty-handed after I would find myself as the only one in the garden. And then...

One day in the *Spring* of 1991... three hundred years after Persephone had slipped from my grasp...

An angelic humming caught my attention, and my mind traveled to Persephone. I sneaked closer, peeking at the owner of the lovely voice as I watched from the shadow of a tree. There she stood: *The Queen of Serendia.*

Kimberly Blake was the spitting image of Persephone, except her falling curls had a chocolate brown shine, but those honey-brown eyes shone like glittery suns, exactly like Persephone's.

In my absence, Zeus had formed a bloodline that would take the stand as *Royalty*, as my years had been occupied with the venturing to the *Elysian Gardens* and back.

In the shadows of the nights and days, I hid and watched Kimberly with desperate eyes. The *Harvest Moon* rose exactly three hundred years after my wedding night with Persephone, and it was on this night I found my solution to bringing a child to Persephone.

I made a blood curdling decision. Like diving into *Dark Blood Magic*, I knew this to be wrong, but the longing in me burned stronger than my grip on sanity and reason.

From afar I watched the king venture away from the property of the *Royal Blake Family*. In shame and dismay, I looked upon a world that had changed from an ancient and respected culture to a world of what people would call a modern kingdom, where even the simple man was equal to the king.

In the royal bedroom, Kimberly prepared for a restful night. In a green misty cloud, I appeared in front of the royal bedroom.

Taking a deep breath, I drank a vessel of blood, and my appearance turned into the features of the king. I grabbed the doorknob, opened the door, and stepped into the room. Kimberly had a wide, beautiful smile on her face at the sight of her husband.

"My Queen," I said with the voice and appearance of Hugh Blake.

I placed my hand on her rosy cheek, silky and warm to the touch, exactly like Persephone's. I gazed into her honey-brown eyes, and for a moment I would have sworn it was my Persephone.

I laid with the queen that night as thunder roared over the residence, and lightning flashed down like the wrath of Zeus.

The balance of life, nature and deities was broken. I had broken the one rule that no God could ever break: *Don't meddle with life on Earth.*

Satisfied, I stood by the window and observed the storm raging outside. Rain impinged on the glass, and the powerful thunder shook the ground.

In the reflection of the window, I could see the satisfied queen, and when I looked at my own reflection, it was not the image of the king that I saw.

It was my own face, but the man I gazed upon was not the man I used to be. Something deep inside of me was intoxicated by the sensation of overpowering strength. The darkness had latched onto me, and in that moment, I was not sure I would ever let it go.

The queen gasped at the revelation that it was no longer her husband who was her company. "Who are you?" Kimberly whispered with terror in her voice.

I turned from the shadows as my green eyes shone. Another crash of lightning lit up my pale face, and a crooked smile formed on my lips. "I am the righteous *Ruler of Earth*... And with the child you now carry, a new legacy will be born."

Wrapped in covers, Kimberly placed a hand on her stomach.

Green mist formed around me as my smile widened, and I vanished. Lightning flashed across the darkened sky as I stood on the balcony of my Temple.

Silently the *Graeaes* approached me, and I glanced over my shoulder. Pemphredo stood in front of the ladies, Enyo on her right and Deino on her left.

"Hypi... The balance of life and deities has been broken..." Pemphredo stated. "What have you done, Hyperi—"

"Call me Sire!" I demanded."

Pemphredo's eyes shone with anger.

"I gave you shelter, I fed you and loved you... Like you have never been loved before..." My voice raised.

"You are right, Sire," Enyo stated.

"I apologize, Hype—Sire," Pemphredo said unwillingly.

"We will stand beside you, wherever you go!" Deino insisted, bowing her head, which satisfied me.

WWord reached Zeus quickly about the daughter of Hyperion growing inside of the Queen. An anger greater than time possessed Zeus as he requested me to stand before him. A faded red light shone from Zeus's white cloak, reflecting on the shining white surroundings of *Olympus*.

He scratched his silvery beard and looked upon me, his formal green-dressed brother. "You stand before us, a traitor of the rules, and our own brother!"

I watched my brother with resentful eyes. "Rules..." I shook my head, viewing the gathering. "You stand before me, brother... the spitting image of *Kronos* himself."

Zeus narrowed his eyes at my statement. "You have been sentenced to rule *The Underworld* until the end of time. You will take the place of Thanatos, the God of

Death, who will accompany you with your tasks of delivering the souls to their rightful places."

"You talk about rightfulness. We are Gods. We are the creators of the rules; are we not held above them? I am Hyperion, *Ruler of Earth*," I demanded.

"Not any longer... You have been sentenced, and there is no reversal of such. As for your name, you are no longer Hyperion.... You are Hades, *Ruler of The Underworld*. You are never to set foot on *Earth*, and you are not to show yourself here. Your punishment is greater than the confinements of *The Underworld*. You are destined to live without warmth or kindness, only to watch as people above you thrive in the warmest of days," Zeus ordered.

A hollow laugh escaped me as I narrowed my eyes at the mighty Zeus. "I go where I please!"

I held out my right hand as a ball of green fire formed. I tossed it toward Zeus, who deflected it back to me. The force pushed me violently back. The air escaped my lungs as I crashed into a white column, which cracked upon my impact.

"You hold no power over me, brother!" Zeus shouted.

I stumbled to my feet with narrowed eyes. I reached my arms out to the sides as a ball of green fire formed in both my hands.

"Hades... Enough!"

The balls fired toward Zeus. He deflected one of them to his right, and the other was deflected back at me. Once again, I flew across the room with a greater force. As I hit the column, the cracks traveled upward, and the column crumbled down upon me. Zeus placed his hands on his back and bowed down his head.

"Take him away!" Zeus ordered the group of black cloaked men, who pulled me from the rubble and seized me. I did my best to fight back. My eyes pierced through Zeus as they overpowered and dragged me away.

"You will see me again, Brother!" I shouted.

"Shelter the child's location!" Zeus ordered, which made me struggle harder to get free.

"You cannot do this, Zeus! She is *my* daughter!" I shouted even louder.

Zeus turned his back on me.

With a loud roar, I broke free from the Gods. A flaring green light shone from my eyes, and black smoke rose from my feet. My heart pounded as I sensed a rush of burning power. My green clothes turned dark, my skin turned grey, and my black shining hair withered to a crunchy grey as a long, bushy beard flowed from my chin. My eyes shone with the brightest of greens, and hatred painted my face.

"You will see me again, brother!" I vanished in an ashen-cloud.

I appeared at the ground of my Temple.

A searing sounded beneath me, and to my horror, the grass burned away underneath my feet. I stepped toward the stairs, and every step I took burned through the solid stone steps.

I reached the top where Charon opened the doors for me. I stepped through and was met with the sight of my beautiful *Graeaes.* They swarmed around me, devastated by my appearance.

I wrapped my arms around them and touched their silky skin, which left them screaming. Like acid, my blackened handprints burned through their skin and spread like wildfire, infecting their beauty with rot, decay, and death. And in the matter of moments, their appearance would never be the same.

"No, no, no... My beauties!" My voice choked with my cries, and I stepped heavily outside and looked to the sky.

"Zeus, this is your doing!" I screamed at the top of my lungs. "You will pay for this!"

A light beamed down in front of me, and Zeus's white figure towered before me. A heavy warmth spread inside of me at the sight of him. He slid a rough hand over his silver, shining beard. His magnetic blue eyes pierced me.

"No, this is your doing, brother!" he stated with all the authority he held. He pointed his finger at me in dismay as his white toga gown flowered around him. You broke the rules," Zeus raged. "You traded your soul for the dark powers. You were too blind and desperate to see the true consequences of your actions. So now you will pay, and sadly this fate falls upon your subjects as well."

A rumble roared from the ground and shook the core of my once beloved home. I turned in terror to see my Temple breaking apart.

I grunted at Zeus. A green ball of fire formed in my hand, and Zeus's eyeroll made my heart pound stronger. The fireball grew in size, and I threw it at him. He deflected it with one hand. I grunted louder.

"Give up, Hades!" Zeus stated.

I created another fireball, throwing it at him. This time he did not deflect it but caught it with both hands. The fireball changed into a white light, and it expanded.

"You doomed yourself, not I!" Zeus demanded throwing the fireball at me.

It hit me with such force that it knocked the air out of my lungs, and I was thrown into the rubble of my Temple. I stumbled to my feet to find that Zeus had retreated to his hiding spot at *Olympus*.

I rushed inside. The *Graeaes* lay on the floor crying at their darkened appearance. All that remained was the shine of their purple, green, and blue eyes.

I bowed down. "My beauties... I will fix this. But right now, we need to get out!"

I grabbed Pemphredo's now-boney hand and helped her to her feet. The other two followed, and Charon gathered beside us. A shield of green light formed around us, and I beamed us outside. And we watched as our home crumbled into rubble and ruins because of the curse I was now placed under.

"Our home..." Deino cried, and she had a hard time standing on her feet.

"I will be your home, my ladies." My gaze fixed on the darkened cave that led to *The Underworld*. I sunk into the darkness of *The Underworld*, cast-out and abandoned.

The crooked, slimy cave walls were now our home. Cold and murky waters flooded around me, like the rivers of my own despair. We had been downgraded to creatures who fed on the blood and flesh of the innocent. The only light was the green torches of shame that I burned for my beauties to see their prey.

Their beautiful eyes gleamed with sadness, and I was the only one to blame for their agony.

From the foot of the rubble and ruins of my former home. My *Graeae's* were now creatures of the night, crawling in the shadows, devouring the blood and lives of the innocent, and those they left behind were turned into monsters in the shape of humans. Blood devouring *Lamias*

» *(Vampires)* who, like their creators, crept in the shadows and deprived the blood and lives of the ones who were ever so unlucky to encounter them.

Cold of heart and empty of a soul, I sat in my stone throne and counted the hours, plotting my revenge.

I sat alone in the shadows for nine months with my *Graeaes*, who were now demised to decaying creatures of darkness and sorrow, as my only company. Their skin was infected by Devil's Drill, white squishy worms, living in bloody circles, eating them alive. Even though the loss of my soul had robbed me of my emotions, there was still a tiny piece inside in my heart, which saw the beauty within the ladies.

Charon was ordered the *Ferryman of the Styx*, to sail souls to my new prison. *Thanatos* would wield his spear and force the tormented souls into even more pain.

Serendia, however, was provided with new protectors: Poseidon of the Seven Seas, who was able to control Air and Water; and Hermes, the God of Luck, Fertility, and Language, who controlled Earth and Fire.

Zeus watched as the *Split-God* baby grew within the queen, and Kimberly gave birth to *my* daughter.

I watched the sun rise and dive, replacing itself with the moon, in an endless cycle of torture. Days melted together, flowing into weeks, then months and years.

Eight seasons came and went. During that time, I sensed myself slipping further and further away from the man I used to be. That handsome man was turned to a man of darkness, and I longed for the days when my visions would come true and my handsome self would return.

In the year of 1993 peace settled over Serendia. My absence had made them secure, and they sensed that their kingdom was safe again.

In the arms of Queen Kimberly, *my* little princess slept as the *Myth of a Dark Split-God* reached their residence. The realization of who their daughter was had spread to various corners of *Earth*, and from that moment,

The Secret was created.

*E*ven though my daughter had been born into the royal family, her location was sheltered from me. My hunt for her began on the night of *The Rare Blood Moon Eclipse*. The Red Full Moon engulfed my *Earth* in a carpet of a red faded light.

I stepped out of the shadows of the *Olympus*, standing before Zeus.

"Frater..." » *(Brother)*.

I spoke in the dreaded language of *Raky*.

"I see you have yet again broken my rules... Speak English!" Zeus ordered.

"Oh, but why... I love the way *Raky* tastes in my mouth." I licked my lips and threw him a crooked grin with narrowed eyes. "Where is she?"

"Of whom do you speak?" Zeus pretended not to know.

"I request what is righteously mine, Frater! *My Earth* and *My Darkness*..." I requested with authority. "You may have hidden her away, but her heart is linked to mine. I can feel her..."

"I see your issue..." Zeus moved closer. "However, I cannot allow you to roam freely in *The Overworld*. You broke the rules, and you must suffer the consequences!"

"She belongs to me!" I fired back.

"A child does not belong in *The Underworld*," Zeus stated. "She is with her family, and they will provide for her greatly," Zeus assured with his hands behind his back.

"Your arrogance is boundless, Zeus!" I hissed. "You leave me no choice. I will stop at nothing to get her back, and the blood of the innocent will be on your hands!" I raged, pointing at Zeus.

"I see the darkness has only corrupted you *further*. As long as I see to it, she will be protected from your destroying grip. For you were the one who truly stole the life and beauty of your beloved *Graeaes*... Were you not?" Zeus mocked.

My eyes narrowed at him. My black cape flashed behind me as I disappeared. In the magical shade of the Red Full Moon my step did not affect my *Earth*. Cloaked in a dark hood, I ventured toward the *Blake Cottage*, strolling through the town of *Hestia*.

People fled, dropping to their knees in prayer at the sight of the *Dark Ruler*.

To my upmost joy, I had disrupted their peace once more. I left the city as flames rose from the roofs, and people cried out in pain and sadness, which only made me grin.

I reached the *Blake Cottage*, and to no surprise my child was not found within its walls. But someone else was.

The flicker of flames danced in the fireplace, and a woman sat in an armchair with a book. Her dark hair framed her face as sterling eyes focused on the pages before her. She had not heard my careful steps approach.

"Nadine Blake."

The book fell to the floor in her fright. She stepped away from the chair and placed both hands on her chest.

"Who are you?" she asked in a shaky voice.

I ignored her question and stepped closer. "You have something I seek," I explained, followed by a hoarse laughter. "Where does your precious granddaughter live?" I lifted my chin, and my green eyes gleamed in the light of the flames.

"Hyperion?" She gasped.

"No." My head shook, and I corrected her. "Hyperion died a long time ago... I was reborn as Hades, *Ruler of The Underworld*." A title I had once dreaded was now declared with pride.

"I will never reveal the location of my granddaughter!"

"Oh, tsk, tsk... So fierce... Do you really think I do not possess the power to take that information? I was only trying to act civil. We are family after all." I threw her a crooked smile. "I do not need you to *tell* me where she is. I need you to *show* me." I approached her, grabbed her by the neck with my right hand, and placed my left on her cheek. She whined in terror.

I closed my eyes and looked into her mind. Memories of happy and joy filled family members flashed through her mind. In the midst of family lay a beaming baby girl.

"There she is... My precious baby girl..." My eyes flashed open, and I looked at the horror in hers. "Well, I no longer need your assistance." I pulled a knife and slit her throat. Blood splattered across my face as she fell to the floor, the crimson liquid oozing from her open neck. The knife glistened in the fire light, and blood glimmered on the blade. My tongue licked across it.

"Mm, sweet and mild. Definitely a good vintage; it has really fermented very well." I dried my hands and face in her silky white curtains.

In a green cloud of smoke, I appeared in front of the *Blake Residence of Sycamore Hills*. Lights shone from every window. My eyes spotted the queen in a window, and a warmth entered my blackened heart.

"I sense you, my darkness... Do not worry, I am coming." I snuck up to the house, waiting.

The Red Full Moon beamed over the house as the lights turned out in one window after another. I hid in the shadows, who were now my friends.

The king and queen slept peacefully as I approached the crib, and there she was. A beauty like that of my *Graeaes.* My flesh and blood were finally within my reach. She adjusted her little hand, and there at her little right wrist was the mark of *The Hectanians.* A tiny black lightning bolt indicated the mark of the ones with power greater than most.

I reached my hand down toward her little cheek. I touched the softness of her raspberry skin and was infected by an electric pain, similar to the agony I felt when my soul left my body. I fell back and hit the wall behind me and crashed to the floor.

The irony was... I could not touch her.

My darkness cried her lungs out, and light revealed my presence. Hugh bolted from the bed and tried to reach me as Kimberly gripped the baby in her embrace.

That was the last time I saw my daughter for years before I vanished in a rush of green...

I waited patiently for a second chance to approach the Blake residence. New measures needed to be taken, and a new approach crafted.

I stood in the entrance of *The Underworld* with my right arm held high. The claws of my new trusted alliance tucked into my arm as it landed, puncturing my skin. Its black eyes looked at me as it shook its blue feathers and peacock tail. For the past dozen months, this beautiful creature, my *Blue Falcon*, had been my eyes to spy on the Blakes. Its golden beak glistened in the sun. With a deep breath my eyes closed, and the bird showed me what it had seen.

The Blake residence appeared in my sight. A wide, yellow-toothed smile spread on my face as I watched the strong protectors of the family leave the house. The ignorant Queen rocked my baby back and forth. Hoarse laughter escaped me before I had even realized.

"Now is the time... My little blue friend, let us visit the royals..."

My eyes watched the white clouds as I stepped out of the shadows. The bird lifted off, showing its majestic wingspan. The grass hissed as it withered underneath my feet, and with a crooked smile, I stepped past the ruins of my temple, continuing determinedly.

Lightning flashed across the sky and crashed in a beam in front of me. Smoke rose from a circle of burned grass, and as the light faded, Zeus stood before me. He tilted his head to look at the withered trail behind me.

"You should tread more lightly... You will not hide in the shadows of the *Blood Eclipse* this time. You have broken my rules for the last time!" Zeus lifted his right hand toward me. "Motus!" » *(Movement with force)*. Zeus ordered as I sensed a pull through me.

My body flew across the valley and through the entrance of *The Underworld* with such force that I could not fight it.

Zeus lifted both his hands toward the mountain that stretched before him. He stepped closer as I watched from the crooked floors of my prison.

"Adducere sursum autem murus de alligatum. Facere non fiat aliguis effugium ac tenebris!" » *(Bring up the walls of confinement. Do not let anyone escape the darkness)*. Zeus commanded in the language of *Kyra*.

I raised myself to my feet, narrowed my eyes, and stepped toward him. But something kept me back. I was blocked by an invisible wall which prevented me from stepping out.

"What have you done?" I roared.

"Taught you a lesson... of what happens when you break my rules. Now you are truly condemned to roam in *The World of the Dead*. Rest now, my brother, among creatures as dreadful as you. Fear not for Delia; she is safe now without any reach of your destroying grip." Zeus's eyes gleamed with accomplishment, and a fire of anger burned inside of me.

I tried for countless days to break down this wall. No force or spell would allow me to exit this prison.

I would wander on the bridge of the Styx staring endlessly into the fiery stream of the Fire River. The flames of the fire river burned as strong as the fire of anger within my darkened heart.

My hand glided over the fire as flames licked my fingertips, and even the pain did not shake the guilt and despair I felt.

The screams and cries from the tormented souls in The River of Sorrow screamed louder than my own inner demons, and I did not know which was worse. The million cries around me, or the one dreadful cry within my darkened soul.

The resigned souls in The River of Woe flooded carelessly with the streams, and it was as though each doomed soul held my face. I squatted down, reaching my finger to the water, as they dipped in it burned like acid. A soul clung to my hand, and I gasped as the despair of a thousand souls rushed through me, stealing my breath. If this were what it felt like to die, than perhaps it would all be the same.

One night I nearly threw myself into the Lethe River of forgetfulness to forget all my torment and pain. How lucky could one be, to forget their sorrows and mistakes? My hope was lost, my visions had turned to nightmares, and there was nothing left for me...

But then the *Graeaes* gave me a gift that would hold my answers. In the depths of the darkness Pemphredo, Enyo, and Deino held out the *Ancient Blood Magic* book, its front torn from the destruction of my Temple.

I grew desperate. The Blakes had stolen my child, and I spent most of my days staring at the pages of the dark book. In the dancing shadows of the green flames, I observed my creatures.

"Pemphredo, Enyo, and Deino come to my side," I ordered firmly yet calmly.

"Yes, sire," they sung in a joined choir. Their beauty had been deprived from them, yet their angelic voices remained. Pemphredo's purple eyes were the first set that looked at me with equal longing and wonder. Enyo and Deino shared a look, which in the faded cave created a shining mix of blue and green.

"I am grateful that you brought this book to me... I am certain our answers will hide inside of this." Their gleaming eyes moved up and down in a nodding gesture.

"Certainly, Sire," Pemphredo stated.

"Your faith is ours," Enyo said in a nod.

"Thanatos, bring out the feast for my ladies." The ground vibrated as the tall frame of Thanatos stepped toward their feeding circle. Over his scar-filled shoulder was the corpse of a man. He swung it around with strong arms, and it hit the ground with a loud terrific thud in the candlelight of the green flames.

I frantically flipped open the book. The dusty wrinkled pages slid across my fingers with each flip. One horrible image after the other flashed before my eyes. Symbols of pain and torment. And then...

A skull with a crystal eye on its forehead was drawn on the page. Symbols and drawings of the *Death Beetles* surrounded the inscription of different spells.

Scribbled in the bottom right corner was an ingredient list. As my hand slid across the page, my fingers caressed the lines of the ink. A rush of relief entered me.

It was a device that would give you sight beyond ordinary understanding. On the other side was a symbol, *The Seal of Sight*, and some writing:

The all-Seeing Sight Instructions;

Do _not_ allow The Sight to fool the mind. everything you see is what has happened, what is happening and what will happen.

The Sight runs on the blood of the creator, none other than the bloodline of thee, can wheel the power of sight.

It sees everything within Past, Present and future. It cannot affect time.

The Sight span has no limitations with the three realms, granting the keeper the gift to look beyond time and distance.

My eyes lifted to the beauties before me, and for a moment I could hardly breathe.

"Ladies, I believe I found our solution."

They lifted their heads from the shredded meat, and with curious eyes and blood covered mouths they approached me. I turned the book in my hands, and their eyes fell on the page, almost illuminating it with their shine.

"I present to you *The Spell of Sight...* With these objects I can craft a device which gives me the ability to look beyond our *Underworld.* It allows me to look beyond our walls and take a peek into *The Overworld* and *The Dreamworld*, the world beyond that what has yet to happen. With this I will have a tool to find pawns to play out my plan. Soon my beloved daughter will return, as will your beauty, and we will take back what is righteously ours!" I stood from my throne with pride and ordered the ladies out to hunt for the needed objects.

In a circle of skulls and wax candles, I sat down with the book in front of me... and waited. Minutes turned to hours. The shadows drifted on the crooked cave walls as time slipped. In the dancing shadows from the candles, I fiddled with small crystals on the ground within my circle. Four pieces in different shapes glistened in my hand. I placed my other hand on it.

A faded green light shone in my hands. I removed one hand which revealed a silver pendant with crystals shaped like an angel.

"The beauty that is Delia..." A smile curved on my lips as I shoved it into the pocket of my black cloak.

My stare was directed back to the black cave walls. Drips of water echoed as I sat in the darkness of my caves, desperately awaiting the return of my *Graeaes*. I studied the spell over and over.

A pitter-patter on the crooked cave floor made my eyes lift to the entrance, where my ladies entered.

"Sire, everything you requested," Pemphredo stated.

"We scoured the deck of Charon's ship and found all your desired pieces." Enyo placed a black cloth within the circle, revealing the contents: a hollow Smokey Quartz, a Herkimer Diamond, and Gold.

I placed the gold lumps in a small metal bowl which stood over flames. The gold slowly melted. Cuts and scrapes spread on my fingers, which quickly healed each time, as I tried to assemble this piece. I assembled the Quartz and Diamond, took the handle of the bowl, and poured the gold around the stone to keep everything in place. My skin seared as the burning gold touched me, but I didn't even flinch. As everything was put together, guilt gripped a hold of me.

"Ladies... I have asked so much of you through our time together, and here I am with a request bigger than anything I have ever asked of you. The power of this tool will only reach its potential with a sacrifice..."

"Whatever the sire needs, we will provide." Enyo nodded, and the shine of her green eyes expanded my inner void tremendously.

"I need.... *The Soul of An Innocent*... and since you ladies have been the purest and most innocent, I have ever had, I will have to request one of your souls." The words weighed heavily on my cold, blackened heart. Even without a soul, I cared deeply for my *Graeaes* who looked at each other for a few seconds before Pemphredo stepped toward me.

"My sire, you need not request anything from us; what you need, we will provide. We will gladly give you not only one of our souls, but all three of them which will represent what you seek: *The Sight* of The Past, The Present, and The Future." Enyo and Deino nodded along with Pemphredo's statement.

"If the darkness of the shadows wishes to claim us even further, then so be it. We have faith that our sire will restore what life, beauty, and soul we once possessed," Enyo assured.

I held a silver dagger toward her. She took it and looked into my eyes. I held *The Sight* toward her. She lifted her rotting, left hand and held the blade to her other. She made a deep cut, and blood dripped down on the stone. She turned and handed the dagger to Deino who repeated her process, and so did Pemphredo. The ladies searched my eyes.

"Repeat after me." An echo sounded like a choir of angels as we chanted the spell:

"Ego exolvo mea dusé pro reditus autem nový vita. Solvo mea dusé tobé." » *(I give my soul for the return of new life. I release my soul to thee).*

The flames flickered as the ladies gasped.

A purple mass rose from Pemphredo. A green from Enyo. A blue from Deino. The colored masses entered the device, and colored lines appeared along the Herkimer Diamond, representing each of my ladies. My eyes scanned all of them before they fell on the device.

"Now for the final step, *The Revival Spell*." I took the dagger, made a cut in my hand, and dripped it onto the device. I closed my eyes and chanted the final spell:

"Per quod imperium de Inferis, Supra Orbis et Somnium Orbis. Ego zebrat pro imperium de podívaná. Nóxium mihi per imperium mimo ordinarius porozumeni." » *(By the command from The Underworld, The Overworld and The Dreamworld. I beg for the spell of sight. Grant me The Sight beyond ordinary understanding).*

The flames blew out, and a multicolored light shone from the device.

"Ladies, I present to you *The All-Seeing Sight*." Their eyes widened, and a crooked smile spread on their pale lips.

"With this... I am... no longer confined by the boundaries of Zeus." My eyes lifted to the ladies, who awaited my next move. I was deeply impressed by the powers within *The Sight*. Leaving me with a wonder about this new power, that was now... Finally, within my reach.

Six

THE CIRCLE
OF SACRIFICE

"Let us see how this works." I drew in a heavy breath and slid my hand across the wrinkled page. The ink-scribbled letters stood out like a cuneiform, waving across my skin.

"Otevreno vision tuum, Ukáz mi facie tua!" » *(Open your vision, show me your sight).*

A strong pull rushed through me, and I sensed myself being dragged forward, like I was pulled down the side of a mountain.

"Ahh!" A searing pain sounded from my forearm. I pulled away the black robe's sleeve to discover a symbol burned into my flesh. *The Seal of Sight* presented itself as a bloody scar, and a connection was crafted between me and *The Sight.*

My eyes squeezed tightly, and in a gasp, I sensed myself fall. My eyes flashed open, only to see the same crooked walls of *The Underworld*. In a sigh I turned and stumbled back. I tilted my head as I watched myself sitting in the candlelit circle with *The All-Seeing Sight* in hand and closed eyes.

I reached out my hand, trying to touch the image of myself, however my hand went right through. As I looked down, I discovered the same device in my hand. And it was then I realized that *The Sight* had created a copy of *The Sight* and that I would be able to walk in the shadows of a new world.

Demeter's cruel remarks crept forward in my mind: "*Shadow God...* Traitor to your own kind."

I squeezed my hand around the device. I bowed down to check the pages of the book.

The Circle of Sacrifice.

The altar of where your Sight will be active, each activation takes a sacrifice, and the Sight will burn itself into flesh. To bring your body to the circle, speak the words of command – Sacrificium.

I cleared my throat, gazing upon the device, and stepped to the entrance of my prison. Hesitantly I watched the grass on the other side, and with another deep breath I stepped forward and right through the wall that had kept me trapped.

A faded yellow mist surrounded everything around me, and the sun was half shaded by the moon which presented everything in a state of black and white. Silence consumed me, and as my eyes dropped to the ground, the grass showed no effect of my step.

"Sacrificium." » *(Sacrifice)*. A rush of wind blew across my dark mane, and I found myself in front of a stone circle. Seven barrel-sized stones surrounded a larger one which stood in the middle. Trees surrounded this clearing; however, these trees stood out in white and grey colors, as if life had faded from them long ago.

As I moved closer, the symbol of Erebus presented itself in the middle of the stone. I rolled up my sleeve, comparing the symbol on my arm with the one on the stone. I carefully placed *The All-Seeing Sight* onto the symbol, and instantly a shiny light appeared and out flew a purple, green, and blue light.

The purple spread to my right, illuminating a symbol on the stone to my right, symbolizing *Future*. The green light beamed to the left, illuminating yet another symbol which symbolized *Past*. And lastly, a blue light fleeted forward, illuminating the stone right ahead of me, symbolizing *Present*.

I gazed at the beaming green symbol. "Show me the moment I met my heart's desire!" I commanded.

The ground vibrated beneath me, and suddenly my grey surroundings blurred as everything came out of focus. It was as if time and space ceased to exist for just a single moment. Everything faded together. Then a sharp white light blinded me, and as it faded, I saw before me my beloved garden in all its beaming colors. And then sounds chimed in the burbling of streams, chirping of birds, and the rustling wind in the tree tops.

And there she stood, just as beautiful as the first time I had seen her. I approached her.

"Persephone." I spoke clearly, but she did not answer. She did not even look my way.

I moved closer as her honey-brown eyes looked my way, yet it was as though she was looking right through me. I reached out my hand to caress her cheek, but it went through like air. Yet again I found myself unable to touch the one I loved so deeply. And in that moment, I realized just how much I would do to break this curse I was under. To win back my wife, bring my daughter home, and restore our life on my beloved *Earth*.

The wind played with her auburn hair, and something within my heart died; the last good piece in my darkened heart was beating for her. Suddenly, I realized that a black smoke was closing in on us, and it was me infecting this beautiful memory. I closed my eyes in deep breath, sensing my body being moved. As my eyes reopened, I stood once again in front of the stone circle, and a warm tear sneaked down my cheek. I quickly dried it off, looking to my right.

The beaming purple symbol was luring me closer, yet I hesitantly observed its taunting light. The ancient scriptures clearly stated the cost of looking beyond. The future held certainty, and what you saw there was what would unfold; your outcome would never be altered. I was not certain I dared to see what kind of defeat I might face.

I restrained myself, looking ahead to the beaming blue light. "Show me the location of the king, Hugh Blake," I ordered strongly, and then everything blurred again.

In a number of minutes, I found myself right in front of the house of *Sycamore Hill*. The huge letter *B* towered over the door and stood out like a welcoming to me. In this state, my presence would not be revealed. Not unless I wanted it so.

The door creaked open and down the three steps walked Hugh, the mighty king. He had clearly aged over the many years I had been trapped by the darkness of The Underworld. His broad shoulders would have seemed frightening to many, as he stood in the wooden doorframe. His suit clung tightly yet flatteringly around his figure.

His brown eyes stared ahead of him with an intense gaze. He ventured to the right of the house and stepped into *The Memory Forest*, and I followed behind.

The air danced in his perfectly combed hair; his hand slid over his hair to keep it in place. He stopped abruptly, looking over his shoulder, which caused me to pause in my step. He shook his head and continued on. As he walked through the green surroundings, he kept a steady look over his shoulder every now and again.

I followed closely, and a twig broke underneath my step. Then he stopped and turned all the way around. *He had heard me.*

"I sense you, show yourself!" Hugh ordered.

"Step into the shadows," I commanded.

Hugh looked bewildered as the yellow mist formed around him, then his narrowed eyes fell on me. "You!" Hugh recognized me.

"Oh, you remember me. That makes me so joyful... Motus Mea!" The power of command left my lips. "MOTUS MEA!" I repeated, but still nothing happened.

Hugh circled me. "Hmm..." Hugh laughed viciously. "I guess your power over me will never come." He lifted his hands toward me. "Motio!" he commanded, and I was forced to my knee.

I bowed my head down in a deep breath. Suddenly his voice appeared inside my mind.

"You are nothing, you are weak... My will shall never fall to yours..."

My green eyes lifted to him. "Oh, you just made your first mistake... You let me in!" I drew in a deep breath, and like with Nadine Blake, Hugh opened his mind to me.

A brief glimpse of images flashed before me: *Hugh ordered a protection on Delia after my first encounter. Then Hugh sat around a huge, long table with his brothers, Kevin and Nicolas, along with a trusted friend, Eric, and a young boy with a spread of ancient papers in front of them.*

"Get out of my head! Akro Motus!" A beam of power flashed at me and knocked the air out of my lungs as I was sent back into my body in *The Underworld.*

A warm liquid ran from my nose, and as I dried it, crimson blood painted my hand. Everything smelled damp and enclosed, and the familiar dripping of water angered me. I grabbed a skull and threw it across the cave. It hit the crooked cave wall, and splinters traveled in countless directions and pierced through Deino's skin and ripped her bloody.

"My lady…" I rushed to Deino's side and held her face, where blood ran down her cheek and tears followed. "I am sorry, my beauty; can you forgive me?"

Silently she nodded as my face frowned with guilt and sadness, and the sudden sense of emotion surprised me.

I looked deeply into her eyes. "They will pay for everything they have done to us. They should never have banished you here; you thrive in the sunlight of *My Earth*. I will make this right, I promise you!"

I stepped back into the *Skull Circle*, grabbed the ancient book, and flipped the page. I looked at *The Spell of Sight* on the left page, and then my eyes wandered to the right page that connected to *The All-Seeing Sight* as well.

I turned the page, discovering a line at the back side of the spell:

Pravilad de quod Visus musí být kratíste aut patior omnes homines. » *(The Rules of The Sight must be obtained or suffer the consequences).*

Anger possessed me as a heaviness sunk upon my chest.

"Sire, what is wrong?" Deino softly asked.

"I broke the rules... *The Rules of The Sight* must be obtained or suffer the consequences..." I turned toward the ladies as my green eyes gleamed with rage.

"Perhaps you should rest, Hades, since you have only just encountered this device and still do not know exactly how it works..." Pemphredo stated. "It is your blackened soul that leaves your body in the physical world. It takes a lot of power and strength, and each time it leaves a physical mark on the body." Pemphredo stepped forward, reached out and held my arm, and slid her fingers around my *Sight Seal* scar.

I ripped my arm away, and a shocked look formed on her decaying face.

"I cannot rest when I know what is at stake... The beauty of you ladies and the life of my daughter!" I flipped back to the spell page and grabbed my dagger, about to make a cut in my hand.

Deino grabbed my hand, staring at me with her shining blue eyes. "Sire!" Deino spoke with a tone never heard before. "You must have a plan!" she insisted.

I ripped my eyes from the power of hers. "Let go of me, Deino!" I raised my voice.

"I will not!" Deino insisted, and Pemphredo cut in. "Sire, perhaps—"

I lifted my hand, stopping Pemphredo in her words. "You do well in knowing who is above all of you!" I viewed all of them and made a cut in my hand. I squeezed tightly around *The Sight*; another *Sight Seal* burned into my arm. My nose wrinkled by the burn, but I closed my eyes and took a deep breath. "Sacrificium."

I sensed the familiar rush through my body, and as I opened my eyes, *The Circle of Sacrifice* stood before me yet again. I placed the device on the middle stone, and the same colors spread out before. I turned my eyes to the blue beaming light.

"Show me past events of Hugh Blake, a few days prior to when I encountered him."

The blurring occurred before me, the vibrating ground pulled at me, and suddenly I found myself in a dimly lit study. Hugh sat behind a desk, and his brothers, Kevin and Nicolas, sat in red armchairs in front of the desk. Eric stood beside Hugh.

All of their eyes directed my attention to the young boy with a black beanie at the right side of the desk, sitting before a spread of ancient papers.

"Delia must be protected at all costs which is why I appointed Eric the sole protector of Delia's life... And I hope that you, Reid," Hugh's attention turned to the young boy, "can find some answers in these old scriptures, so I can keep my daughter safe!"

My blood boiled by his statement of MY daughter.

"I am extremely pleased that you have been willing to study languages with me," Nicolas told Reid. "It gives us the upper hand, that someone who is as ordinary as you will have such power," Nicolas suggested proudly.

Power? What is this talk of power? I wondered as I observed the skinny little fragile boy. He was their big hope in translating the *Ancient Hectcraft* and *Ancient Blood Magic.* I closed my eyes and whispered, "Odhalit mysteria."
» *(Reveal your mystery).*

When my eyes reopened, a misty light rose from each person in different colors, where their most desired wishes expanded, and their *Thought Voices* rose to my attention.

"*Delia and the family's protection are the most important.*" A cloud of blue symbols danced above Hugh's head.

"*I must rise to the respect that Hugh sees me reaching.*" Eric smiled lips as green beetles flew around him.

"*I have to prove my worth to the ones above me. My brothers have seen me as nothing but a little jokester boy who can't accomplish anything.*" A glow of a yellow light gleamed from the boy. Looking at Kevin and Nicolas, a similar yellow light gleamed from them. A gleam of hope and wonder of what they truly sought was deeply hidden. Only a personal visit would show their desires. A smile spread on my lips as my eyes moved to Hugh.

"Let us see how well your plans work, Hughie boy!" I closed my eyes and felt the rush pull me back to *The Circle*. I observed the colors in thought. "Hmm... Going after Eric right away would be foolish. He obviously got great power since he is appointed guardian over *my* daughter's life. Let us see who this Reid truly is..."

I closed my eyes and drew air in through my nose. "Motio." As I reopened my eyes, I stood in the corner of a room, hidden in the shadows.

The boy sat at a desk, he could not have been a day past sixteen, and he were their huge solution.

He wore a hat that covered most of his blond hair and was deeply occupied by stacks of papers laid in front of him. The language of *Raky* spread across the pages.

A deep laugh left me as I tilted my head at him. "Reid..." My ominous whisper caught Reid's attention.

He looked to his left and listened. My whisper lured him out of his room as he followed the sound toward an oval mirror which hung on the wall.

"Closer, Reid..." My whisper grew more intense as I watched him from the frame of the mirror.

Reid noticed me in the mirror with a green mist around me.

"Who the hell are you?" Reid wondered, tilting his head.

"The one who can answer all your prayers." Reid looked around in the room and shook his head. "You want to prove your brothers wrong, do you not?"

His eyes flashed back to me. "How do you know?" Reid wondered with a shaky yet curious voice.

"What if I could provide you with the abilities to learn the language of *Raky* and *Kyra* in minutes?" I offered.

"In minutes... Impossible," he stated in a skeptical voice.

"Let us make a deal... All you have to do is provide me with a single word," I stated as excitement prickled in my fingertips.

"A word? What word is that?"

"Ano." I fought a smile as his eyebrows frowned.

"Ano? You mean yes?" Reid's face turned bewildered.

"Spustit!" » *(Activate)*. The colors of the room turned to the familiar yellow mist.

Reid lifted his head and looked around in confusion. I stepped out of the shadowy mirror. Reid stumbled back and fell into his chair, and then he dropped to the ground and pressed himself against the chair.

"Motus Mea!" A powerful force lifted him from the ground and moved him to me. I placed my right hand on his chest and my left hand on my own chest. "Cavea Nobis. Svázat!" » *(Ground us. Tie us)*.

Reid gasped as his pupils expanded and retracted, and his stare went stiff. He took a step back and stared at me.

"What am I to you?" I failed to hide my excitement with a satisfied smile.

"Sire, *The Ruler of Darkness*..." Reid spoke in a hypnotic tone with a blank stare.

"What will you do?" The authority in my voice was shattered by unwilling laughter.

"Everything you desire!" Reid stated numbly.

"Good... Show me your mind." I reached into his mind where everything was covered in darkness, and only a tiny, shimmering light was lit in the middle of this despair. An incredibly young boy sat crying.

With a deep breath, I opened my eyes and looked at Reid. "Your mind is weak. How you store such knowledge on language, I do not know. Do you pretend to know these crafts, or is this all just a ruse to seem better than you are? Regardless... Go back to your papers." I snapped my fingers at Reid, and he turned around, leaving the room like nothing had happened.

That was almost too easy to take the will of a child which suits me. Perhaps I hold the power to look elsewhere, perhaps even the little right-hand guy. His powers will hold nothing against mine.

Seven

POSSESSION OF POWER

I watched Reid one final time before I closed my eyes and sensed how I was pulled back to *The Circle*. A sense of accomplishment flowered inside of me, and this kind of emotion seemed foreign to me. The victory I had over Reid's mind made me confident in winning over Eric as well. I viewed *The Sight* on its resting place on the stone, and my eyes moved to the beaming blue light.

"Bring me to the location of Eric Stevens."

The pull of time sucked me in, and I found myself in *The Memory Forest*, surrounded by rows of white trees. As I looked back, I realized how deep into the forest I was. The *Blake Residence* was a tiny white spot at the end of the forest trail.

A whisper came to my attention, and I gazed ahead. Eric strolled before me in the greyish surroundings. His black, greasy hair was combed back, and his green eyes directed his way as a black coat blew behind him. He vanished in an entrance of bushes on his left, and I followed.

A stone circle emerged in the middle of a clearing with a huge rock formation in the middle. *The Circle of Sacrifice had a ground here in the Overworld.*

He stopped at the foot of the stone circle. A bubbly sensation entered me from the thought of what I could do next. I circled around, reached out and grabbed his shoulder. An electric burn pierced my hand, and I dropped the device. As it hit the ground, I awoke instantly in my physical body. I growled in annoyance. *The Graeaes* watched me with wonder.

"Sire, did it work?" Enyo softly asked.

My eyes quickly flashed to her. "No, it did not. The beastly thing burned my hand, so I dropped the device and broke the connection..."

"I warned you, Sire... Your mind may not need rest, however your body does!" Pemphredo hissed through sharp teeth.

"Watch your tone, Pemphredo!" I ordered, standing up within the skull circle.

"She is not mistaken, Sire..." Enyo softly added. "You need to recharge."

"How will I find means to restore myself within this hellhole!?" I shouted. "There is no means of power!"

"Oh, but you are wrong, Dark Ruler," Deino insisted, taking my hand in hers. She guided me to the dark, crooked cave walls. She placed my strong hand on the clammy surface, laying her thin and boney hand on mine.

"Energy of a million souls is oozing from these walls." A beaming power filled my hand with a burning tingle. "We all have faith in your ability to bring us home, however this will only happen if you play it smart. We have been stuck here for years. What are a few more moments if it will allow us to leave this place?" Deino's blue eyes shimmered at me.

I bowed my head down. "You are right! If I cannot beat him, I have to cheat him... I will befriend him enough to gain his trust, and then I will steal his control." I took her hand into mine, looking into her blue eyes. "Thank you, Deino." I placed a humble hand on my chest.

I lifted my chin in revelation, and a new idea occurred. *I could not appear as myself. I have to take the appearance of someone else, like I did with Hugh the night Delia was conceived. But who?*

"Ladies, I have a plan." A wide, yellow-toothed smile spread on my white lips, and my new plan created a sense of satisfaction.

I nodded to Deino, bowed down, and took the book. My eyes glided over the crooked surface of the cave walls, and suddenly I saw my prison differently. It was no prison, but a vessel for me to grow stronger. Smokey Quartz stood out from the walls in different shapes and sizes, and within each a little green *Soul Light* burned. Thanatos would state that these were like souls he was fondest of, so he kept them.

"My beauties, I must travel to the town of *Hestia.* There I will find the one who will help my plan unfold." I smiled at my ladies who gathered before me, bowing their heads respectfully and silently praying for me to save their lives and beauty. I held *The Sight* tightly as another scar seared into my skin from the activation of the device.

I stood in the square of *Hestia.*

The town had shifted in form and size over the many centuries, and an unfamiliar world was beckoning before me. Modern they called the new ages, and people rushed by carelessly, not having any trouble in the world. They minded their own business, going about their daily lives. The city was loud with people rushing from store to store, greeting each other.

Some of the roofs were blackened from the flames that had tried to suck away the life of this town, and still people seemed to have forgotten as quickly as it happened. I was claimed to be evil, but it was those who did not mind about other's lives or the demise of nature, who were truly evil in my eyes.

Suddenly, I felt a push at my shoulder, and a guy rushed by me, shouting an apology. A sense of belonging and familiarity echoed within me, and I watched him in wonder. *Had he seen me and touched my shoulder? How could this be?*

I followed him to a store on the corner with glass windows all the way around. Cosmic Corner was written across each of the windows in cursive writing. I looked through the glass door and saw that he stood by the checkout. I stepped through the door as if I were made of air. His eyes lifted when I was almost all the way in front of him.

"Oh, good evening, sir... Sorry I bumped into you. I must have lost my head there for a while..." The clerk offered, looking at me with green eyes while his dark hair and features reminded me of myself.

"You see me?" I wondered.

He stopped what he was doing, surprised by the question. "As clear as night!" The bewildered look on his face did not fade.

"Night?" I repeated. "Normally, one would say *day*, would they not?" I suggested.

He shrugged. "Well, I am not one... I am the other. People pretend to fit in, pretending to be something that they are not..." He stated.

"I believe your heart is as darkened as mine!"

"Excuse me?!" The clerk took offence at my words.

I took one step closer, looking into his eyes. "I believe you house darkness. You may not know it yet, but your future will hold wonderful things," I offered. "Why do you believe that you could see me, when no one else could?"

"Because I have eyes like most people!"

His statement made me chuckle. "But clearly, you see things much differently... What is your name?" I wondered.

"Blackwell, Laurence Blackwell..." He said proudly.

"My, my... A forceful name: *The sacred darkness*." I nodded to myself in amazement. "Laurence, let us make a deal."

"What kind of a deal?" He wondered skeptically.

"You are certainly no fool." I smiled. "What if I could offer you a trusted eternal companionship? You swear your legions to me, and I will offer you protection and a family that will never turn their backs on you."

"What is the prize?" Laurence wondered in a serious tone.

I held up my right hand, and *The Sight* dangled in its silver chain. "You simply allow me to live within your body once in a while. And then... you will never be lonely again. You will be surrounded by beauties and loyal companions... You will be a part of *The Darkened Ones*. All you have to do is swear your alliance to me and offer me a vessel of your blood." I made my offer, and Laurence fell silent as he considered. *And it was then I realized that even the loneliest and most desperate souls could so easily be pushed to the dark side.*

He reached his hand out to me. "Deal!"

I took his hand and shook it. Then I placed my knife and a small glass bottle before him. He created a cut in his hand and dripped blood down in the glass bottle.

"You will be the first of many! Oh, and by the way... Do you by any chance know the Blake family?" I wondered.

"Yes." Laurence nodded as he wrapped his hand in a white cloth.

"Marvelous!" A wide smile spread on my lips.

"So, what happens now?" he wondered.

"Now, I play out my plan... You, however, will live your life as you always have. If you need anything, I will know it, and if I need you, you will know too." I accepted the glass bottle from him and nodded. "Thank you again, Laurence," I offered before I vanished in a cloud of green smoke.

That night I slept soundly for the first time. *Somehow my wishes and visions had changed. What if I could have everything of both worlds? Rule the darkness of The Underworld as well as proudly ruling over my Earth? Delia and the Graeaes would fill our home with beauty and love, and I would control those who would stand against me by confining them within the walls of hell. Persephone would return to me, and our lives would be complete.*

My eyes flashed open.

I rose before my ladies, holding Laurence's blood vessel in my hand, and I looked upon each of them.

"Today is the day that our lives are going to change. And we will be one step closer to everything we ever wanted…" I shared and a crooked toothed smile spread on all of their lips. I grabbed my knife and made a cut in my hand.

"Otevreno vision tuum, Ukáz mi facie tua!" » *(Open your vision, show me your sight)*.

A searing scar burned into my flesh yet again, and the familiar pull of gravity took possession of me. In a rush of power, I stood before *The Circle.* I placed *The Sight* determinedly into the symbol on the middle stone, and looking beyond to the familiar blue shine, I drew in a strong breath.

"Show me Eric Stevens!"

The powerful rush went through my body, and when I opened my eyes, Eric walked around the *Circle of Sacrifice.* I lifted the blood vessel, removed the cap, and took a sip of the blood. My appearance shifted and changed to that of Laurence. My eyes shone like his green beads, his checkered red and orange shirt wrapped itself around my features, and his saggy pants felt uncomfortable. I touched my chin and scratched my stubble. Then I looked upon Eric who stood with his back toward me.

"See me..." I whispered and beaming colors of nature spread around me: green, brown, and orange. Creaks of twigs revealed my presence.

Eric turned around, looking at me in bewilderment.

"Who are you?" Eric asked with suspicion.

"Laurence Blackwell... I was told by Gavin that you are the one to come to about *Ancient Blood Magic*," I started. "I discovered that speaking loudly of such ways is very frowned upon, however I heard you practice this, and I wondered if you could be of assistance?"

"How do you know of that craft?" Eric asked, still not falling easily into my trap.

"My mother... She practiced *Hectcraft* in *Melas*... Sadly, she died before I could ever learn from her, so you are my last hope." I tried to sound as pathetic as possible.

Eric looked at me suspiciously for the longest time, and my heartbeat accelerated. My clammy hands circled around each other.

"Who did you say sent you here again?" Eric wondered with piercing eyes.

"Kevin!" I exclaimed.

"I thought you said Gavin," Eric suggested.

"Well, I mispronounced..." I chuckled nervously, drying my hands on the uncomfortable pants. "*Kevin* spoke highly of you... He stated that you specifically would be able to tell me about the *Blood Magic*."

"Laurence... Laurence..." Eric spoke, tilting his head. "Do you own *The Cosmic Corner*?"

My heartbeat calmed. "Yes! That I do..."

Eric curved his lips in a nod.

"Alright, well I do not regularly dive into *Ancient Blood Magic*, but I guess I can make an exception," Eric offered with a smile.

Could he really be as powerful as they said, when he was so easily fooled?

"So, what do you want to learn about this *Hectcraft*?" Eric asked as we sat down on one of the stones from the circle.

"Well, I am not even certain what there is to learn about the craft," I lied, finding it hard to fight a smile.

He chuckled at the statement, which I found hard to understand. "Sadly, there is only one book of *Ancient Blood Magic*, and it was lost many centuries ago."

I was rejoiced by this fact. However much he knew about *Ancient Magic*, there was so much more he wanted to know himself.

"Perhaps you can simply share with me what you do know... It can certainly be more than I do!" I suggested, and Eric replied with a nod. *How could Hugh appoint him sole protector of my daughter when he could not even protect himself from betrayal? He seemed to dive right into my trap, and he was eating the story from the palm of my hand.*

"My schedule is fairly tight today. Perhaps you can meet me at Olysia tomorrow, and I can try to show you some spells and discuss the craft further," Eric offered.

"Marvelous, Eric. I will see you again at Olysia," I replied, and he nodded before turning around to leave the clearing.

I closed my eyes, rushing back to my body in *The Underworld*. The ladies looked at me.

"My beautiful *Graeaes*... He was not suspicious of my appearance at all! I will meet him tomorrow and try to win his trust even further," I said as a trickle of emotions returned to me with pride.

"Excellent!" They all hissed in sinister voices.

For the first time I began to wonder when this darkened place had corrupted my beauties. It was as though a part of them was forever lost. Time was rushing down into the bottom of the hourglass, and I had to convince Eric to trust me so that I could restore not only myself but, most importantly, my beloved *Graeaes*.

That following day I activated *The Sight*, drank a sip of Laurence's blood, and appeared in the beautiful valley of Olysia. Green grass spread for miles, and a wide flight space took up space at the right of the parking spots. To my right, the waterfall rippled hypnotically into the crystal-clear lake, and the wind danced romantically with nature. Flowers rocked gently back and forth, and treetops were shaken to life. *Oh, how Persephone would have loved to walk here by my side.*

"Hello!" To my surprise, Eric approached me, and in my daze, I had not heard him arrive.

"Good day, Eric. I am pleased that you would clear your busy schedule for me," I offered politely.

He nodded. "Alright, I thought I would share with you a bit of how and why *Ancient Blood Magic* was created..." Eric started.

"I mean no disrespect, but I would really love it if we could jump right ahead to the spells. Perhaps you can show me how it works?" I wondered with a hidden agenda.

"Well, of course." Eric nodded yet again.

"I would like to find a balance between creating and destroying so I will know what not to do. When *Hectcraft* builds, *Blood Magic* tears it down, right?" I acted innocent and ignorant.

"Yes... The craft of *Blood Magic* is extraordinarily strong and powerful." Eric squatted down, holding his hand over a white lily. "Concido!" » *(Break down)*.

Eric commanded, and the flower withered away. He lifted his eyes to me.

"How much would one be able to expand that command?" I wondered.

"It depends on the power within..." Eric turned his gaze to the flower, still holding his hand above it. "Restituo." » *(Restore)*.

A beaming light infected the withered flower, bringing it back to its former white shine.

"How much would you be able to expand such an ability?" I tried my upmost to sound genuinely curious.

"Well, I alone would not be able to do much more than taking down a few trees. But in union and connection with others I could take down a whole forest... But as you said, not many want to turn to the ways of *Blood Magic*." Eric shrugged, standing up straight.

"Sometimes people do not see another choice but to fall into such ways..." I hinted.

"That is absolutely true. Sometimes life gets too hard for some people..." Eric looked over his shoulder at the flight space behind us.

"You fly?" I asked, and he turned his eyes to me.

"I used to... A lot has happened lately in our lives, so the flight lessons were shut down. Hugh... The king and I used to serve together in The Serendian Protection Force. I am a flight captain, but most of my time is now spent with..." He paused, realizing how much he was opening up to a complete stranger.

"I did not mean to pry," I quickly stated.

"No, I know. Sometimes it is just hard to talk about... I have this longing inside of me... The sensation I get when I am lifted high into the sky is intoxicating. I miss it..." He chuckled to himself in reminiscence. "Anyway... Today was all about what you needed to learn."

A wide smile snuck to my lips; he was opening up to me in a way he had not intended. My plan was working in my favor.

"If it is too much for you, we can call it a day," I offered, but he quickly shook his head.

"No, it is quite alright..." He tried to maintain focus, but something had shifted in his eyes. And I had now seen his weakness. "I am sorry, Laurence... A heavy responsibility lies on my shoulders, so my mind is a bit clouded today."

"It is completely okay... When my mother died, my mind was clouded for years." I tried to say anything I thought would make him open up further. My insides were turning with excitement, and I was fighting hard not to pull a smile. It was working; his walls were crumbling down.

"I am sorry to disappoint you." Eric sighed.

"Do not worry about it. Perhaps we should meet up again in the town of Hestia. We can go over some of the most used spells of *Blood Magic*," I added.

Eric nodded, and the look on his face revealed how disappointed he felt in himself. He stepped away from the valley, venturing toward the flight space, and the moment he was gone from my view, my true appearance was revealed. I beamed back to *The Circle*, placing *The Sight* on its resting place.

I looked upon the purple light. "Show me Eric Stevens in this very moment!" I commanded. A circled frame of purple light created an image of Olysia.

Eric sat on a bench by the flight space, his head was buried in his hands, and once he looked up, he sighed deeply in despair. He slowly ventured toward his car, driving toward the Sycamore Hills. Once inside the residence, he strolled through the high ceiling hallways. At the end of the hall, he made a turn to the right, entering a room which only held an unstable desk, a single person bed, and a pile of clothes that seemed like it was about to run off by itself.

And in that moment, I realized the loneliness that Eric was consumed by, and I rejoiced yet again. He had nothing, and his whole life's purpose was to gain respect from the king. Pathetic.

The image faded, and a cloud of smoke brought me back to *The Underworld.*

"Soon, my ladies, all our wishes will come true. Eric will be like butter in my hands... I will soon be able to shape him into whatever or whomever I want." The kaleidoscope of their eyes beamed at me with an intrigue I had not previously seen in this darkness.

"Are you certain of this?" Pemphredo wondered.

"Absolutely. He is growing weak. Tomorrow will be the day I trick him and take over his life," I stated with a confidence I had not felt in an awfully long time.

I strolled through the town of Hestia, and I squinted at the *Cosmic Corner* where I had commanded Laurence to stay so he would not interfere with my plans. I walked amongst people who did not see me with a smile on my lips. It was as though my powers were growing along

with my victories. First Reid, then Laurence Blackwell...
Now Eric, and sooner rather than later, I would control
the life of Hugh Blake.

A young lad caught my attention by Demeter's
Paradise. A park presented in her honor, if they only
knew what kind of Goddess she really was. I wrinkled my
nose in disgust.

He ventured inside, and I followed. Yellow flowers
sprung ceaselessly, and life streamed in this park. It was a
shame that no one knew of Demeter's true side; perhaps
they would have named this garden something else.

The lad stood by one of the sprouting trees. I snuck
up behind him, whispering, "Meduse!" » *(Turn to stone)*.

He choked, fighting to catch his breath. A smile
spread on my lips as he turned into a greyish statue.

I glanced up at the white statue of Demeter on top
of a fountain.

"A few more of these and your garden will have
stature" I cackled, turning around, and exiting the garden.
I took the vessel of blood out of my pocket and drank the
last mouthful.

"Vyjít!" » *(Come forth)*. I ordered. Colors spread
around me and the city sprouted with sound. And on the

corner of *Ashen* and *Cozy*, Eric walked. I approached him; he looked so oblivious.

"Good day, Eric... I am certainly ready for new things," I stated as he pulled a faked smile.

"That certainly sounds good." Eric continued down the street, and I followed behind.

I made sure I was a tiny bit behind him as I whispered under my breath, "*The Circle.*" A cloud of green smoke swallowed us, beaming us to the ground of *The Circle of Sacrifice.*

"What is happening?!" I tried my best to sound frightened.

Eric looked around as the cloud faded. He turned his back toward me, observing the circle before us. When he turned, I was standing right in front of him, holding my right hand at his chest and my left on mine.

"Cavea Nobis. Svázat!" » *(Ground Us. Tie us).*

A green shine flew from my mouth and into his. His green eyes glowed as my power entered him and then widened as my appearance changed back to myself.

The power traveled down Eric's body; my eyes fell on a silver skull ring with crystal eyes on the middle finger of his right hand. A glowing green light shone from the crystal's eyes as if there were green flames in the skull.

With a crooked smile, my hand moved from his chest. His brows curved as he looked down, discovering the shine in the eyes of the skull. His shocked gaze returned to me.

"What the hell did you do to me?" Eric's brave voice had vanished, replaced with fright.

"Grounded and bound us. You will never escape the reach of *The Sight*." I lifted the device above my head with satisfaction.

"To you I am Sire, *The Dark Ruler of The Underworld*." I tilted my head as I observed him.

"What do you want?" Eric's voice grew more demanding.

"Only your collaboration... Let us make a deal! You obey my every word, and I will spare your life."

"I would rather die!" Eric stated bravely.

"Well, you do not have a choice." I shrugged, curving my mouth downward.

"I know you..." Eric's eyes narrowed in reflection. "Hades! You are nothing but trouble, and I will do everything I can to protect the Blake family and their baby girl," Eric insisted.

"*My* baby girl! You hold no power over me, pawn!" I raised my hand toward him as the *All-Seeing Sight* dangled from its chain in my hand. Eric was forced toward me, and my right hand settled above his heart while my left hand rested above mine. My eyes stared into his. "Perhaps I should do a little test run on you," I declared and looked down at his ring.

The green eyes of the skull gleamed as I smiled. My hand lifted toward him, and I drew in a satisfying deep breath. "Být mea autem." » *(Be my tool).*

Eric mechanically, stepped backwards, and sat down on the wide rock behind him. I stepped forward.

"Alright, Eric Stevens... Now tell me, who can or will be in my way?"

His eyes squeezed together. "No one... No one knows of you, besides Hugh." Eric tried to fool me, which forced great laughter out of me.

"If you were wise, you would not lie... I know who knows of me... The sweet and beautiful Kimberly knows me. Nicolas and Kevin... and who else?" I lifted my head in thought and patted my chin with my pointer finger.

"Nadine... oh no, that is right. I killed her.... Who else? Oh yes, Madelin Blake and Hermil... of course before he died himself..." I paused and looked at Eric. "How did he die again?" I wondered.

"I don't know," Eric said vaguely, another lie.

"More lies... *Verum*..." » *(Truth)*.

A light changed in his eyes.

"He bequeathed his abilities to Delia. She and Kimberly were endangered... Therefore, he gave his life to save Delia," Eric explained mechanically.

"That righteous scoundrel." I placed my hands at my sides and turned my side toward him.

"There is more..." I ripped my eyes back to Eric. "They created a *Healing Blockage* on her, to protect her from you. They are building a fortress of protection around her. They will do everything to keep her safe..." Eric mocked.

"Let us see how long that lasts!" I paced around in wonder. "What else should I know about my obstacles? What about Reid Cohen; what can you tell me of him?"

"The nephew of Kimberly. He has been studying with Hermil, the dark language of *Raky* and the powerful language of *Kyra*, known by very few," Eric shared unwillingly.

"Hmm, but how good is he really?" I pried.

"Very good... He is a jokester of another world, but his intelligence is boundless; he learns extremely fast," Eric insisted with a serious look in his deep green eyes.

"Hmm, we will see..." I suggested with confidence.

"What about Hugh?" Eric wondered, surprised.

"All in good time," I said, not sharing my plans.

"How about Josh, the oldest of the Blake children, a nice way to be close to the family and Delia?"

Eric's suggestion made me laugh.

"Oh no, he is too weak of mind for me to possess." I cackled at his vague suggestion.

"We will see about that..." Eric said in a low voice but still meant for me to hear. I ignored him.

"So, tell me... What is the mighty king's weakness?" I wondered with a mind full of ideas already.

"His wife, his children, and his family," Eric stated.

"No, I mean what will make him reckless, not thoughtful or considering? Who does he?" I stopped in the middle of my words and gazed at Eric with a sinister look. "How much does he trust you?" I asked with intrigue.

"Enough!" Eric's voice rose with authority.

"You are a witty one, hm? Will he trust your words and perhaps nervous behavior?"

Eric lifted his shoulder and straightened his back. "What is your plan?" Eric fished for answers.

"A game of surprise." I walked to him and held my hand over his head. I closed my eyes. "Prijit!" » *(Step in)*.

As I opened my eyes, I saw everything through Eric's eyes. He was back in the colors of the physical world, and his eyes watched the residents of the Blake house. Eric was in a mental battle as he tried to push me out and fight against the grip I had on his mind.

Through my eyes in the *Shadow World*, I followed behind Eric as if I had become his shadow.

As I stood behind him, I moved my head closer to his and whispered in his ear, "Enter!" My sight was his as he entered the residence. "Now, my pawn, go find my next target! Bring us to the king!"

With reluctant and heavy steps, he ascended the stairs and walked around a hallway.

Door after door passed by until he finally knocked on one of them. My heart pounded as a mimic of his.

"Come on in!" A deep voice sounded from the other side of the door. Eric's hand shook as it reached for the handle and turned it open.

"Eric? Did you forget something? Hugh Blake sat behind his desk with perfectly combed hair. He wore a suit and had a questioning shine in his brown eyes.

"Now arrange a meeting with him in a place of peace... Tell him to meet us there at twilight!" I ordered with a warm breath on Eric's ear.

He looked to the side in disgust, shifting his focus to Hugh, who tilted his head.

"Eric, are you alright?" Hugh wondered with deep concern.

"I have a proposal for you, sir. I have... I have seen some issue at the flight space of *Olysia*... Perhaps you can meet me there at twilight," Eric suggested with a small shrug.

"Twilight? What is the issue about?" Hugh gently shook his head in confusion.

"You will see, sir... I just need you to trust me," Eric insisted with a nod.

"Okay, I will meet you there," Hugh said suspiciously and nodded as well.

Eric turned around, left the room, and closed the door. As he descended the steps I whispered again in his ear, "Good, little pawn. Now you will walk until you reach *Olysia*, and there you will sit on a rock and wait for twilight. You will see me again, Eric!"

I closed my eyes and left the connection with him. I stood by the entrance of *The Underworld* caves and looked down at *The Sight*.

"Výnos!" » *(Return).*

I closed my eyes tightly, and with a gasp, I reopened them. The gleaming eyes of my *Graeaes* watched me as they held their breaths.

"Did it work, sire?" they wondered in despair of what to do with themselves if my plans would not work.

"Indeed!" I nodded with a satisfied smile. "Hope is no longer lost for us, ladies."

I stood in the entrance of my dark caves and watched the sun slowly crawl over the sky as nature danced gracefully in approval for the day to end. As the twilight colors danced in the sky, I looked down on *The Sight* and cut into my hand as another *Sight Seal* appeared on my forearm.

In the yellow, misty black and white world, Eric sat on a stone near the *Olysian Lake*, staring into the air, but as he saw me, his eyebrows curved in an angry frown. Just as I approached Eric, a car crunched on the gravel of the parking space nearby. Eric's eyes widened slightly, and he seemed to have an inner battle with himself for the control I held. Out from the car Hugh stepped and trudged toward Eric.

"What was the problem?" Hugh wondered.

"I must war—"

"—Quiescis." » *(Stop).*

My command rendered it impossible for Eric to utter another word. "Step into my world!"

Hugh looked around in wonder as the colors vanished, and yellow mist consumed him.

"Your Majesty." My words made him turn in reflex, and I place my right hand on his chest and my left on my own. "Cavea Nobis. Svázat!" » *(Ground us. Tie us).*

Hugh gasped as the green light entered him and turned his silver wedding ring black. I grabbed his neck hard and held my head to his ear.

"You belong to *me* now! There's nothing you can do to stop me from getting my daughter!"

Terror screamed from Hugh's eyes, and he looked to a powerless Eric, who could not even move from the stone. An unwilling laughter spread all the way from my stomach. My eyes met with Hugh's as a tear drifted down his cheek. I stared intensely into his soul.

"Drive home and give *my* daughter a kiss from me."

Abruptly Hugh turned around, walked in a trance to his car, and drove off.

I laughed again and turned to Eric. "Sict!" » *(Leave)*. I ordered, and Eric raised from the stone.

"You are as cruel as they say... You really think Delia will be happy with you in *The Underworld*?" Eric waved his arms to the sides.

"On the contrary, she will not be living with me in *The Underworld* because with my power I will take back what is rightfully mine... *My Earth*..." I waved my arms upward to present my wonders, "and my beloved Delia... *My Graeaes* and I will craft a world with both sides of *Raky* and *Kyra*. A world of *Shadows* and *Light* where my precious child will grow to love both sides. She will not be tainted by the ways of simple men. She is special, she reaches above all else, and she will rule this world long after I perish!"

I reached into my pocket, pulling out a silver chain with the angel pendant which glistened.

"Make sure to give this to Hugh, and make sure it reaches Delia.... And remember, I will be watching you!" I handed him the necklace with a wide smile.

With my newfound power, I now controlled the lives of Hugh Blake and Eric Stevens. Through their eyes, I watched my daughter grow. I gathered information, that could provide me with a way of holding my daughter.

At last, my plans could unfold.

Outro

Many stories tell this tale. But many are wrong. This I know, for I have seen the truth. Through these journals I discovered the truth about my true father. Finding my father's journals was what inspired me to do the same, to write my own.

My life began in a cloud of darkness, secrets, and betrayal; this I came to know in the hardest of ways.

I am Delia Blake.

The daughter of Hades.

TO BE CONTINUED IN ONLY HAYDEN.

THE AUTHOR

Maria Ashen is a Danish/English Fantasy author, whose admiration for writing brought her on this journey of writing her own book series. Ashen uses her troubled past to create loveable and realistic character.

FOLLOW MARIA ASHEN: